BOOMLAND · Hale

BOOMLAND

BY

Jane Hale

Cover Art
by

LaShelle Oursbourn

A Rainbow Publication

*"At the end of every rainbow
is the promise of another good book."*

International Standard Book Number
ISBN 0-934426-20-1
Library of Congress Catalogue Number
LCCN 2003090429

PRICE: $12.95
(plus $3 shipping if ordering from publisher)

Available from:

Rainbow Publications
45 Rocket Road
Buffalo, MO 65622
(417) 345-7759

try our web page at
www.firecrackerlady.com

Printed in the U.S.A. by

Stewart Printing & Publishing Co.
Route 4, Box 646
Marble Hill, MO 63764
(573) 238-4273

DEDICATION

- *Boomland* is dedicated to my family, who for years have spent Independence Day in a fireworks location providing the public with merchandise to celebrate the Fourth of July.

• For my dad, Blaine Shewmaker, and my mom, Inez Sadler Shewmaker, who introducd me to fireworks sales.

• For our sons, Rick, Reg, Mitch, and Lucas, who grew up with the fireworks business. To their wives, respectively, Karen, Gai, and Suzyn, who married, not only a husband, but a fireworks job. And, to our grandchildren, respectively, Blaine, Nathan, Zachary, and Chase, Cali, Colby, and Nick, Chayla, Austin, and Jacob, who are the fourth generation of fireworks vendors at Hale Fireworks, L.L.C.

• And, to our extended fireworks family, who spend Independence Day selling product and join us at the end of the summer for a bang-up celebration

Enjoy!

The Firecracker Lady

Table of Contents

Author's Notes

Boomland, fourth book in the 'Land' series of holiday mysteries should have been a snap to write. My family owns and operates Hale Fireworks, L.L.C., with retail outlets in five states. But when I started writing, I found myself trying to educate my readers about the fireworks industry instead of moving the plot along.

As I eased up on the firework details, a haunting sixty-year-old mystery began to unravel. I wondered if the next book in the series, *Spookyland,* was in progress. I relaxed and kept on writing and was amazed to find not one mystery but two emerging as Thomas and his family opened their fireworks tent on a farm in Branson, Missouri.

As Independence Day drew near, so did a stalker, who was dead set on doing harm to Thomas and his dog, General Freddie Freedom (GFF).

The public kept buying fireworks and the mystery kept evolving until *Boomland* blasted into a bang-up finish just in time for the Fourth of July.

Once again, LaShelle Oursbourn illustrates a super cover, Ellen Gray Massey lends support as editor, and David Stewart performs his magic as a printer.

Rainbow Publications lives up to their motto once again: "At the end of every rainbow is the promise of another good book."

Enjoy!

Foreword
The History of Firecrackers

Although Black Cat® fireworks has been a registered trademark in the United States for fifty years, the real history began in China.

It all started with the burning of bamboo sticks, which made crackling and loud popping sounds. The people believed the noise would drive away evil spirits. The Chinese logic quickly discovered evil spirits were pernicious, resilient creatures who could not be permanently scared off. If it was desirable to fire bamboo and set light to crackers at Lunar New Year, for the sake of health, harmony, and prosperity, then why not at weddings, anniversries, and many other events in the life of people?

It was from this the fireworks industry was born. For more effective crackers producing color as well as noise, chemicals such as potassium perchlorate were mixed with metal salts. And there were endless permutations and combinations possible. These gave birth to the highly exotic and versatile industry it has become today.

Fireworks are universal and the vivid display of exploding colors in the night sky gives delight and pleasure to people of all ages in the United States where fireworks have been used for years to celebrate Independence Day.

Shiu Fung Fireworks and the Fung family, who own Li & Fung Ltd., help support fireworks safety education through donations to the SPS and NCFS. They are pleased to have Black Cat® fireworks mentioned in Jane Hale's children's book, "Boomland."

Through courtesy of
Ralph Apel
President of Golden Gate Fireworks, Inc.

Foreword

A Word from the Fire Marshall

Fireworks have been around our country for centuries dating back to the first inventions of black powder, used by our ancestors to fight against their enemies or used as an explosive component to build railroads, bridges, roadways, and buildings.

Throughout history we have learned the use of fireworks is to recognize something of celebration. Our Independence Day is the first celebration that comes to my mind, but there  are many other celebrations fireworks are used for. Young people and older people are all amazed at the joys and bright colors of our fireworks today, lighting the sky with numerous colors and loud noises, making those in attendance admire the wonderful celebration.

Safety with the use of fireworks is always the very first thing to remember and share with others. Through years of the use and making of fireworks, safety and handling have been the utmost of importance to the user. Even very minor accidents, while using fireworks, can put a quick damper on the celebration of the day and cause pain and discomfort, at times even more serious.

We have learned throughout our history how to handle fire in a safe way and not a harmful way. In the early days, the use of a controlled fire was found to help us cook our food, warm our home and make light during the darkness hours. When a fire gets out of control, disaster can occur very fast, burning homes, buildings, forest, and many times humans and animals. By using anything that has an open flame in a safe environment, always using safety while around others, making sure that our homes and surroundings are safe, will make our celebrations enjoyable and less harmful.

William Farr, Missouri State Fire Marshall
Office of the State Fire Marshall
State of Missouri
1709 Industrial Drive
Jefferson City, Missouri 65109

About the Author

Jane Hale lives in Buffalo, Missouri. She and her husband, Bob, have four sons and ten grandchildren. She is an active partner in Hale Fireworks, L.L.C., in five states: Missouri, Kansas, Louisiana, Mississippi, and in Bentonville, Arkansas, where they really do have a company doing business as Rainbow Fireworks. The graphic shown below is Hale's private label for a

 shell named in her honor, *The Firecracker Lady.* Many of their fireworks have labels named after members of the Hale family.

Since 1999, she has written an award winning weekly column in Buffalo, Missouri, *The County Courier,* " Buffalo . . . As I Remember It!" in the voice of her childhood, Little Janie Shewmaker.

She is a free lance photo-journalist having credit with major publications.

Hale owns and operates Rainbow Publications and Toys. Under her direction a program, "Recycling Reading," was devised to benefit school libraries. As author of the 'Land' series of holiday mysteries, Hale visits schools to discuss writing and publishing with students. Her books are available at reduced prices. A portion of the sales go to the school library to help recycle reading and purchase test discs for her books through Accelerated Reading (Renaissance.)

The first four books in the 'Land' series, *Wonderland*, Christmas mystery, *Heartland*, Valentine mystery, *Foreverland*, Easter mystery, and *Boomland*, Fourth of July mystery are available on-line at Amazon.com, Barnes & Nobel.com, Published.com, and in local bookstores. Or look for the order blank at the end of this book.

Order Mollycoddles, companion stuffed animals, also. Freddie Freedom is the companion animal for Boomland.

Spookyland, Halloween mystery, and *Homeland*, Thanksgiving mystery, will be available soon to complete the six book series.

Visit www.firecrackerlady.com or email the author at jshale@ripinternet.com.

These words appear on the fireworks box called "The Firecracker Lady," named after Jane Hale.

"Beautiful, classy, consistent, colorful, appears to be everywhere–starting with a tribute to carrying Olympic torch and continuing with a wide variety of effects—the firework is also very impressive."

About the Illustrator

LaShelle Orsbourn teaches art in the Lebanon school district and loves to do illusrating in her free time. She and her husband, Joe, are the proud parents of three boys, Chris, Matt, and Ryan. She treasures her time with her entire family and thanks God for all He has blessed her and her family with.

Chapter 1

Wonderman

Danger! Light fuse and get away!

Thomas Scott blew on the smoldering punk. An ember of fire glowed hot enough to ignite a firework fuse.

"Ready!" He inserted the explosive WONDERMAN load into its shooting tube base.

"Set!" He extended the punk toward the fuse and glanced at his friend, Lefty Tucker, flanked by his collie, 'CC' Colonel Charlie.

"Light it up!" Lefty urged.

"Go!" A tremor of excitement shook his wiry frame as Thomas touched the white-hot punk to the firework fuse.

It sparked!

Thomas cried, "Run!"

CC yipped as he raced with the boys across Rainbow Firework's parking lot at Bentonville, Arkansas.

"Va-room!"

Fireballs soared into the heavens. A flash of color lit up the sky. Millions of lights swirled, forming the giant outline of a super hero.

Thomas sucked in his breath. "Gadzooks! It's WONDERMAN!"

Presto! Another fireball exploded in front of WONDERMAN and became an opponent with weapon raised.

"Earth to WONDERMAN! Get ready to battle!" Lefty yelled.

CC echoed the warning with a yelp.

Bolts of fire erupted from WONDERMAN's extended arm flashing across space to eliminate the enemy, who cascaded downward in bursts of color.

"Right on target!" Thomas shouted.

"Excellent!" yelled the crowd of firework dealers who had been invited to Rainbow Firework's pre-season display.

The image of WONDERMAN rocketed higher and exploded into the outline of a spaceship which soared upward and disappeared into the dusk.

"Yee-haw!" Thomas jumped up and down as he yelled.

"Yee-haw!" Lefty echoed.

CC barked, chasing around boxes of demo fireworks.

"WOW!" Thomas gasped, "I didn't think anything could be as cool as getting to go to Hong Kong on spring break, but having fireworks named for you is awesome!"

"Totally!" Lefty agreed, kneeling to hug CC who nuzzled his knee.

"Good show, Super Hero!" Thomas addressed WONDERMAN, who stared back from the brilliant blue firework box holding the artillery shell kit. The masked hero with hair the color of fire looked proud to be named in honor of Thomas Scott and the word, WONDERMAN, the boy had chosen for his computer password.

Thomas said, "Tonight is kinda like a preview of coming attractions."

Lefty ruffled CC's fur, "Yep, less than a month till the Fourth of July and fireworks. WONDERMAN's plane will be protecting the skies. He'll rank right up there with Red Baron, Chuck Yeager, and Pappy DeMouse."

"Who?" Thomas looked puzzled.

"Since you're a super hero fan you've probably never heard of famous World War One and Two pilots," Lefty scoffed.

"Hey, I've heard of the Red Baron, the Ace who shot down eighty planes," Thomas exclaimed. "I didn't know you were into history."

"I'm not." Lefty lifted the flap on a fireworks case and peered inside. "My grandmother has been briefing me on pilots' names. She's going to mention them at the Fourth of July celebration honoring veterans for Independence Day."

Thomas tugged the corner of one flap of the box. "And?"

Lefty grunted, "Pappy DeMouse, one of the Aces, is going to be on the program at the Ducks Baseball Stadium in Ozark, Missouri."

Thomas's smile flickered bright as the early June fireflies blinking in the Arkansas twilight. "You mean Pappy DeMouse is going to be recognized at the same ceremony as us?"

Lefty raised his eyebrows comically. "Can you believe it?" Lefty pulled the box with brilliant lettering free of the case. "They actually are going to give us an award."

Thomas nodded. "And, we're going to be on the same stage as Alabama and The Ozark Mountain Daredevils."

"And, Rainbow Fireworks is putting on the show!" Lefty boasted. "Can't get much better than that!"

Blinking a mist of proud tears from his eyes, Thomas focused his gaze on his mom, Carol, standing with her husband, Martin, and his daughter, Wendy, and the group of watchers near Rainbow's warehouse.

As if sensing Thomas's stare, Tom Scott, looked toward his grandson and signaled a satisfied thumbs-up approval. He was chatting with TNT, Lefty's grandma, the lady who owned Rainbow Fireworks, and others who, like Thomas and his grandpa, would soon be selling fireworks to celebrate Independence Day.

"Hurry up, Thomas! Shoot another one," Seven year-old Wendy yelled.

Everyone laughed.

"Let's do it!" Thomas urged Lefty.

"Okay, but this time it's my turn." Lefty picked up another artillery shell box with the design of a baseball diamond on it. Brilliant letters formed the word, SLIDER.

"All right! SLIDER'S the fireworks shell named after you. Have you shot one yet?" Thomas asked.

"Nope," Lefty's fingers fumbled at the wrappings as he hurried to unwrap the kit, "TNT said to wait until we were all together. It's kind of a celebration of the baseball episode on the airplane coming back from Hong Kong."

"Remember what the man interviewing us for television news said?" Thomas lowered his voice in a perfect imitation, "It was pretty impressive the way a twelve-year-old and a fifteen-year-old picked off the terrorist on that airplane with baseballs!"

"Yep." Lefty peeled away the cellophane and opened the artillery shell box displaying colored loads in the shape of baseballs.

"Which one, Lefty?"

"They all look good, you chose."

CC nosed a yellow baseball, whined, and looked expectantly at Lefty and Thomas.

Thomas reached for the yellow load and handed it to Lefty. "Okay, in honor of Cackleberry Chick," he said, remembering the Molleycoddles animal, who had become a big part of their FOREVERLAND adventure.

Lefty ruffled the dog's fur. "Let's go!"

They ran back to the shooting area. Lefty handed Thomas the reusable tube from WONDERMAN and replaced it with the tube from SLIDER."

"Be careful!" Carol called.

Thomas waved a reassuring hand at his mom.

Lefty positioned the fireworks tube base securely between two rocks. "Let's do it!"

He lifted the long, brown punk stick and blew on the end.

"Ready?" Lefty watched for Thomas's nod then lowered the yellow ball into the tube. He touched the punk to the fuse. It sputtered and caught fire.

"Scram!" Lefty yelled.

Breathless, Thomas, Lefty, and CC skidded to a stop near the fireworks warehouse and turned to watch showers of brilliance explode into the air.

"Wow!" Thomas shouted, as an outline of lights became a baseball diamond in the sky.

"Way cool!" Lefty yelled, when another blast erupted into home plate with a player waving a bat.

Both boys gazed skyward as a series of explosions formed a pitcher winding up at the mound.

"And now the pitcher holds the ball and now he lets it go . . ." Thomas quoted from a long-remembered poem.

"And the air is shattered by the force of the batters . . ." Lefty prompted.

"Strike one!" A voice bellowed from high in the sky.

CC growled and moved closer to his master.

Lefty's mouth dropped open. "Man, I didn't know fireworks could talk!" He whirled to look across the space at TNT.

His grandma favored him with an exaggerated shrug, mimicking, "Who knows what they'll come up with next?"

Another strike followed quickly. On the third pitch the ball began to break away from the batter as it came closer to the plate. When the batter swung, he missed it by inches for "Strike three!"

Lefty pounded his left fist into his right palm, over and over. "Did you see that, Thomas? The last pitch was my slider!"

"Awesome!" Thomas agreed, dropping to one knee to hug CC, who had been nudging

Thomas's leg. "What's the matter big guy? Feeling left out?"

CC drooled a slobber on Thomas's cheek.

The spectacular show in the sky held Thomas's attention but he whispered reassuringly in the dog's ear, "I wish I had a buddy like you."

The baseball diamond disappeared into popcorn-sized blasts of color to a chorus of "One, two, three strikes, you're out."

"Totally outstanding!" Lefty yelled, running with Thomas toward the watchers, with CC close on his heels. He hugged TNT. "I've got to send Mark McGwire one of these."

"You know Mark McGwire, the baseball player?" Wendy asked.

"Sure, Lefty met him when he was a guest at one of the Cardinal games," Thomas said.

"Wow!" Wendy's eyes sparkled.

"Is it okay if we shoot off some more new firework items?" Lefty asked his grandma.

"Later, maybe. Right now, we need some help getting the tables ready to eat." TNT moved about arranging food on the tables.

Kids carried ice chests and pop. Martin helped Lefty's dad at the grill.

The fireworks crowd milled about discussing the upcoming fireworks season and the effect the dry weather might have on their retail season.

"Can states ban the sale of fireworks because of the long hot spell?" Grandpa wondered as he set the catsup and mustard Thomas handed him on a table.

"Sometimes," TNT said. "You having second thoughts about running that tent in Branson because of a little dry weather, Tom?"

"No way! Thomas thinks our running that tent is the next best thing to winning the boys National Amateur Athletics Union basketball title in Florida." Tom winked at his grandson. "Sometimes I think basketball may come in second."

Thomas nodded and left to help set up extra chairs.

Carol edged closer to Grandpa. "Have you had a chance to remind Thomas what TNT said about age?"

"I hate to spoil his fun tonight. Let him ride to Springfield with me tomorrow. I'll mention it then." Grandpa shrugged. "TNT pointed this age deal out before. Funny how we have a way of forgetting."

"What if—" Carol's question was interrupted by the call to eat.

Thomas, Lefty, and their group wolfed down their burgers in anticipation of shooting more fireworks. CC patrolled their table enjoying bits and pieces of food the kids tossed his way.

TNT dabbed her mouth with a napkin. "UMMM! Those burgers are good!" she grinned at Martin. "I may have to give you a burger contract."

A loud belch sounded from the kids' table. "I believe I've got a second on that." TNT laughed along with her guests.

A siren sounded in the distance and gradually drew closer. A car with a blinking light pulled into the driveway of the fireworks building.

With Lefty in the lead and Thomas close on his heels, the kids emptied their table and headed toward the official-looking car.

The driver's window slid down. A voice boomed from inside the car, "TNT around here?"

TNT hurried toward the car grumbling, "Old Jess Sawyer! What brings an inspector from the Fire Marshall's office out here?"

"We got a call someone was shooting fireworks. I might have known it was you."

"I bet you smelled food, too. Since you're here, you might as well eat." TNT introduced Tom and his family as she maneuvered Jess to their table. "Jess used to run a stand for me and my late husband."

"It's sure kind of you to feed me."

"As if that wasn't what brought you out here in the first place. You didn't fool me with that story about people calling in to complain about us shooting fireworks." TNT's laughter was echoed by others.

"Are we in trouble for shooting fireworks?" Thomas shot an anxious glance in the officer's direction.

"Naw, Mister Sawyer and TNT are good friends. Like she said, he knew there's free food and he likes to talk fireworks." Lefty moved toward their picnic table with a plate of food for Sawyer.

"Fireworks season is almost here." Jess added some more catsup to his burger. "The twentieth of June is less than two weeks away. That's my busy season, too."

"Working for the State Fire Marshall's office, Jess knows some real good fireworks stories," Lefty said.

"Don't encourage him, Lefty. We'll never get rid of him." TNT's warning was softened by a smile.

Thomas moved closer to his grandpa. "Isn't this exciting? Aren't you glad we're running a fireworks tent?" Thomas whispered.

Grandpa nodded.

Thomas turned his attention to the story Jess was telling. He failed to notice the look of concern that settled over his grandpa's features.

Several couples left, mosquitoes were biting, and still the fireworks stories continued.

"Time for bed! Carol's nodding off." Grandpa patted Carol's arm gently. "Mothers-to-be need their rest."

"Just one more story!" Wendy begged, "Mister Sawyer, tell one more."

Jess looked inquiringly at TNT.

TNT shrugged. "Make it quick, Jess."

"Tell us a kid story," begged Wendy.

"Let's see." Jess scratched his head, "Well, there was this time I had to shut down a tent because the parents had left their thirteen-year-old kid running it."

TNT looked quickly at Thomas. Then she stared a question at his grandpa who responded with a shrug. She interrupted, "Er, on second thought, Jess, we better save the stories for another night. Carol does look tuckered out."

The crowd packed up to leave.

"Why would Mr. Sawyer shut down a tent because a thirteen-year-old kid was running it, Lefty?" Thomas asked with a puzzled look on his face.

"Well, Thomas," Lefty began.

But Thomas was already moving toward the man in uniform. "Mister Sawyer, can I ask you a question?"

Carol glanced at Grandpa, who frowned, and shook his head.

"Sure, son."

"How old does a kid have to be to run a fireworks stand?"

Sawyer began to rattle off fireworks law, "In Arkansas no one under fourteen years of age is allowed to sell fireworks."

Thomas swallowed hard. Tears were beginning to form in his eyes as he turned an accusing look on his grandpa and TNT.

Chapter 2
TNT

"I can't work in the fireworks tent?" Thomas's bottom lip quivered. His eyes flared with alarm.

Carol moved closer to her son and put a hand on his shoulder to calm him.

TNT waved at the last car as it drove out of the parking lot. Then she turned to Thomas and Grandpa. "I didn't make the age law. The state did. I bend over backwards to abide by all their laws to stay in business. If they say fourteen is the legal age to sell fireworks I'm more likely to say sixteen." She softened her words with a smile.

Martin eased Wendy over to stand by Carol. He put a consoling arm across Thomas's shoulder. "As a private investigator, I know what TNT means about obeying the law." He nodded as though emphasizing his words.

"But," Thomas started to interrupt.

His mom held up a warning hand.

Martin gave Thomas a consoling hug. "Missouri and other states have employees, like Mister Sawyer, who are responsible for making sure firearms, fireworks, and other related things, are conducted according to their state laws." He paused, as though considering and directed his question to TNT. "Is the age for selling fireworks the same in Missouri?"

Thomas looked up hopefully.

"The laws don't vary much." It was TNT's turn to consider. "If I'm not wrong I believe Missouri wants their people to be sixteen before they can sell fireworks." Turning to Thomas she spoke in a gentle but professional manner, "Thomas, the very first day we talked about you and your grandpa working fireworks, I mentioned the age for selling, remember?"

"Yeah, I guess so. But why did everyone let me think I could work in a fireworks tent this summer?" Thomas's voice was belligerent. "I've told my friends Grandpa and I are running a fireworks tent in Branson."

Lefty broke in, "No one said you couldn't work in a fireworks tent. You just can't sell fireworks until you're fourteen."

"So what can I do?" Thomas shot Lefty a questioning glance.

"Same as I did. Work your way up—restocking, running errands, and watching that people don't steal—"

"There is plenty of ways to help around a fireworks tent," TNT said. "You can put up the red, white, and blue bunting around the tables, string the lights, put up signs, haul fireworks, unload them, display and price them. Lefty's done all that and more."

"Does that mean I'll get to help put up the tent and—"

"I've got a crew who sets tents, but if you and Tom want to help, I'm sure they won't put up a fuss." TNT paused. "Tom, you probably need to make Thomas your manager. He can make sure everyone does their job while you collect their money."

"Thomas, if you're a manager will you make me your assistant manager if I work really hard?" Wendy begged.

"Sure Wendy." Thomas grinned.

"I plan on coming down to help out," Martin said.

"And, Sydney Snyder, my computer buddy from California, wants to come. He's going on down to Florida to watch my basketball team, the Panthers, in the National AAU tournament after the Fourth."

"Okay, son," Carol said, "you just brought up something you need to think about. I'm sure your coach is going to want you at basketball practice if you're *going* to the AAU Nationals. You can't just leave your grandpa without any help."

"I'll help, Thomas. That's what assistant managers do," Wendy announced. "I'll make sure everyone works hard."

"Now that you've got that settled, let's get some sleep." Martin gently moved Carol toward the car. "Wendy, Thomas?"

"TNT, since I'm going to stay overnight with you, is it okay if Thomas stays too?" Lefty asked.

"Thomas can ride back with me," Grandpa offered. "We can go back by Branson tomorrow and check out our location."

"Let him stay," TNT urged Carol. "I guess we'll see you at Ozark at the Commemorative next week."

Carol beamed. "Can't miss seeing our young men get their awards, can we?"

TNT nodded. "Ready boys?"

At TNT's home, Lefty, Thomas, and CC settled in the room upstairs that had belonged to Lefty's dad.

"Looks like your dad played baseball, too," Thomas said, picking up a trophy to read the inscription.

"Yep, but Dad's really into haunts." Lefty handed Thomas a small book with the title, *Mysterious Myths.* "Look at this."

"Your dad likes spooky things?" Thomas asked, skeptically.

Lefty nodded. "Did you know there are haunted places all over Arkansas? And in Missouri, too."

Thomas crawled onto his bed, propped up a pillow, and opened the book, "Did you ever visit any of these places?"

"Yep." Lefty settled onto the other twin bed. CC made himself comfortable near the footboard.

"So, tell me about them."

Lefty switched off everything but the night light. "TNT will be on the phone half the night checking on business. But you can bet she'll be checking on us too."

"Can we whisper?"

"Yep." Lefty lowered his voice and began his story.

"Dong, dong." the big clock in the hallway downstairs echoed throughout the house signaling two o'clock in the morning.

Moonlight crept through the windows outlining the bed where Thomas lay, head covered, eyes peeking from beneath the covers. He listened to Lefty finish what promised to be his last spooky tale, ". . . so, he took the dead dog to the basement. Then he opened the trap door and he and the dog disappeared into the bottomless pit. Years later, ghostly barking sounded from the basement and a woman in white prowled the house . . ."

"Creak!" The door to the bedroom opened a crack. "Boys?"

Thomas jerked beneath the covers.

Lefty sucked in a silent yell.

CC whined, and did a fast dog paddle up to Lefty's pillow.

An image in white glimmered in the doorway outlined by the glow of moonlight flooding the room. "Lefty, do you know what time it is? I bet you're filling Thomas's head full of your dad's haunt tales. Just remember those trucks will be loaded in the morning no matter how much sleep you boys get."

They breathed a sigh of relief as the door closed. They heard footsteps padding down the hallway.

"Man! Your grandma scared me to death," Thomas said.

"Me too." Lefty considered, "I don't know which would scare me the most, TNT on the prowl, or the ghostly woman in white I thought she was."

The boys' laughter rang out in the still of the morning as Lefty switched off the night light.

"Nite, Thomas."

"Nite, Lefty. Nite, CC." Thomas pulled the covers tighter around his head. "Hey, would you leave that night light on?"

"My thoughts, too," Lefty said, reaching for the switch. A soft glow blended with moonlight that filled the room.

Soon youthful snores, mixed with the soft huffs of CC, echoed throughout the bedroom like memories of yesterday.

Chapter 3
Mister Jones

"Rat-a-tat-tat!" Firecrackers blasted continuously as Thomas and Lefty scampered around trying out Hale Bombs, loudest legal brand on the market.

"Come on, Thomas, let's get going," Grandpa called as he finished loading the last of their supplies into his car. "We're going to deliver Mister Jones's insurance policy for the fireworks location."

The two boys sheltered their punks and ran to Tom's car.

"Cool! Can we put up the tent while we're there?" Thomas asked.

Lefty hooted with laughter.

TNT suppressed a smile. "Trust me, you'll want some help with a one hundred by sixty foot tent."

Grandpa chuckled. "We're going to stake out the area where the tent crew will set up the tent. If Thomas wants to help set up the tent, let us know when the crew is coming, and we'll be there." He motioned for Thomas to get in the car and got in himself.

TNT leaned down to look in the window. "I hope you've got your fill of shooting fireworks for awhile. Remember the rule! We shoot fireworks before and after season. Once we're selling we don't shoot any!" The stern look on her face emphasized the seriousness of her words.

"And! No one else can shoot them near our tent," Grandpa said, starting the motor.

"Read your state laws and you and the State Fire Marshall's office will become friends. You're both working for safety with fireworks to make a good holiday," TNT said.

Lefty reached into his pants pocket, extracted a CD and handed it to Thomas. "Download my new security software on your computer. It'll project an image of would-be night robbers in infra-red light on a selected spot on your tent. Wallah! Call nine-one-one! Or turn CC loose on them."

"You're making all this up, right?" Thomas had already decided if Lefty was teasing that he could rig up a system like this on his virtual reality soft wear program, WONDERLAND.

"Afraid not, computer wizard. Your friend, Sydney Snyder—guru of cyberspace—has been aced on this softwear gig."

"I can't wait to get on my computer and Instant Alert Sydney about this." Then, his voice dripping sadness, he said, "But, it won't work."

Lefty eased his head next to TNT's near the car window, "Why won't it work, Brainstormer?"

"'Cause," Thomas's lips drooped, "we don't have a CC."

Lefty whooped, "You're right. Better get you a big-bad-watchdog."

Thomas waved until they were out of sight of the warehouse.

Then, he settled back in his seat, pulled out

a book and began to read.

"What's that you're reading?" Grandpa asked, several miles on down the road.

"A book Lefty loaned me on haunts. His dad really digs this stuff." He grinned at his pun, held up the book, and said, "Spook-tac-u-lar! What do you think, Grandpa?"

"Oh! You want to hear about haunts? You've come to the right person. When your grandma and I lived in Branson on the farm, we lived next door to a haunted house."

"You spooking me?"

"Nope, settle back and I'll tell you a tale or two."

The miles flew by as Arkansas turned into Missouri and still they exchanged haunt tales.

Mid-afternoon they pulled off the highway and into Mr. Jones's field where the tent would be. "Nice wide entrance for all those cars that'll be pulling in to buy our fireworks, eh Thomas?"

"Sure, let's get out and stake off where the tent will be."

Grandpa parked the car. "We've got to take this insurance up to the house. TNT has already sent Jones a check to cover the rent, but you don't start working on a man's property without saying 'hello' first."

Instinctively, Thomas matched his grandpa's steps. The closer they got to Mr. Jones's house the slower they walked.

"Is anything wrong?"

Grandpa's face, awash with evening sunshine was bright, but his eyes were blank—like someone had lit his firecracker and the fuse had gone out.

Thomas stopped walking and grabbed hold of his arm. "Hey! What's wrong?"

Tom blinked. He looked toward an old barn in the pasture. A shudder shook his body. "I'm sorry, boy. I just felt like a ghost walked across my grave. Too much spook talk, I guess."

Old Man Jones opened the door on the second knock.

"Tom Scott? I thought it was about time for you to show up."

Mr. Jones motioned to the rickety lawn furniture on the porch. "Who's this you got with you?"

"Thomas, say hello to my friend, Harley." Grandpa nodded Thomas a reminder to respect his elders.

Thomas extended a hand and grasped the frail hand that felt like he imagined corn husks would feel. "Pleased to meet you, Mister Jones."

Harley considered Thomas. Abruptly, he asked, "Tom, is there any way I can back out on this fireworks agreement?"

Thomas sucked in his breath. A sudden chill prickled his neck. *Someone or something is trying to keep me and Grandpa from selling fireworks.*

As though sensing Thomas's thoughts, Grandpa glanced at him. "I'm afraid not, Harley. If it was just me I might reconsider but Thomas has his heart set on it." He continued in a business-like manner, "Besides, we're independent contractors with a big fireworks company out of Arkansas. Why would you want to back out now?"

"It's awful dry. If those fireworks start a fire the whole place could go up in a matter of minutes."

"Harley, no one will be allowed to shoot fireworks on your property!" Grandpa said with conviction.

Instead of arguing further, Harley asked, abruptly, "Tom, you remember my boys?"

"Just barely. How are they?"

The conversation seemed to be getting back to safer ground, Thomas thought, until he heard the old man's answer.

"I believe one's dead. The other one is God knows where."

"I'm sorry." Grandpa's voice sounded strange.

Thomas felt like he'd stepped into the twilight zone. One minute they were discussing fireworks, dry grass, and fires. Now, Thomas wasn't sure what was coming next.

Harley got up from his chair and walked to the far end of the porch. "It was a long time ago, Tom. See that barn at the back of the field?" He pointed to the ramshackle building that Thomas had seen his grandpa staring at earlier.

"Oh, my sweet Lord! How could I forget?" Grandpa seemed in pain. "I remember now. I used to come to your house with my older brother, Bud, to play basketball. You had the only barn big enough for kids to play basketball inside."

"Bud?" Harley seemed to consider. "Bud

Scott! He was Dave's age. Remember Dave's dog, Booger?" he asked slowly.

Thomas's head was whirling as the conversation twisted and turned into pathways he couldn't follow.

"Sure, a big, black dog." Grandpa's voice had an excited edge to it. "Scared the pants off me the first time I saw him." Grandpa looked at Thomas and blinked as though surprised to see him but thankful for the reality of his image. "I was just a kid younger than you, Thomas."

Harley continued, "My older boy, Mick, never liked that dog. He'd tease him until the poor animal would go wild. It made Dave so mad! Even though Dave was a lot smaller than Mick, he'd chase him with a stick trying to get him to leave his dog alone."

Thomas had a mental image of Lefty throwing CC's stick to fetch. He blurted, "Did it work? I mean, did Mick leave Booger alone?"

The old man studied the question. "No. It never did. But Booger got his revenge the day Dave died."

"Died!" Thomas echoed the word and stepped closer to his grandpa. Could he be asleep? Was he having a nightmare?

"Harley! I swear, I plumb forgot, I'm so sorry. I guess kids just blot out things they don't want to remember."

"I wish I could forget." The old man's shoulders drooped.

When he continued, Harley's voice sounded like it was packed for a long journey. "But that day stands out clear in my mind. A bunch of Dave's friends had come to play basketball. It was getting late." Harley stopped and scratched his head thoughtfully. "Mick was at the table. That was unusual. He's generally the late one. He was always tinkering with cars down at that gas station in town." He paused, narrowing his eyes, like he could imagine the scene. "That night it was like he kept pestering his ma to serve supper." A frown creased his forehead, "Ma rung the bell for supper but Dave didn't come. She sent Mick after him. She never forgave herself for that."

Thomas listened closely, afraid he'd miss the old man's words.

Grandpa rubbed his chin the way he did when he was trying to remember, "How could I have forgotten? I was with Bud that night. Mick came running through the barn hollering at Dave and broke up the championship game."

"They say Mick had a big stick," Harley said. "He wacked Dave, causing him to stumble and his shot missed the goal. Dave got so angry he turned Booger after Mick."

Grandpa's eyes had a glazed, far-a-way look." He rambled, "Mick picked up the stick and started teasing Booger with it. Then, he ran outside to the well." Grandpa stroked his chin, "The old well was out back of the barn. The one fed from a spring where we got drinks of cold water after the game."

Harley nodded absently, "I was afraid there would be trouble and started down to the barn. When I got closer I heard the commotion." His voice went faster matching the action," Dave's friends were chasing after Mick and Booger."

Grandpa's and Mr. Jones's words painted pictures of that long ago day for Thomas. He could see the boys, their dog, and just ahead was some terrible thing he knew was going to happen.

"Dave had taught Booger to fetch a stick," Grandpa said. "Mick used that trick to keep the dog off him. He'd throw the stick and Booger would fetch it. By the time the poor dog would get it and try to bring it back, Mick would have another stick and throw it. Booger was slobbering mad, but he wouldn't stop going after the stick." Grandpa shook his head, "I never seen anything like it."

Harley sputtered his excitement, "Wh-wh-at surprised me the most was Dave. While everyone was out back of the barn, he picked up the basketball and was practicing his free throw shot. Bounce-bounce-shoot, bounce-bounce-shoot! Just as if no one was around."

Harley suddenly turned on Thomas with a crazed look, mistaking him for his son in the long-ago misadventure. "What are you doing, boy? You going to let your brother and your friends ruin your dog?"

Thomas took a hesitant step backward from the crazed, old man.

Harley's mind was in the past as Tom continued with the tale.'

"That's what you said all right, Harley. Dave looked at you and said, "Never, you mind, Pa. Booger will take care of Mick." Grandpa sighed,

"I saw both of you, Harley."

"Did you now? So you were the little boy that stayed inside?" Harley's eyes glittered. "Did you see my Dave change his mind and run outside?"

Grandpa nodded. "Yep! I followed him out fast as I could."

Harley's words tumbled over themselves, "Me, too. I was just in time to see Mick throw the stick toward the well, it arched, and barely cleared the top, landing beyond the well in a clump of bushes."

As though he were seeing the action happen through Dave's eyes, Thomas watched the boy named Mick as he threw a stick toward the well wall. Thomas asked, "The stick, did it look like it went into the well?"

Harley turned to Thomas, once more confusing him with his youngest son, "Yes, you saw just enough to think the stick went in the well. You thought your dog went in the well after it. But Booger followed the line of the throw. He jumped up on the casing of the well, bounded over, and was hidden from our view as he continued hunting for the stick."

"By the time I got outside . . . " Grandpa hid his head in his hands as though he were a small child and couldn't bear to remember.

Harley rambled on as though he'd never heard Grandpa, "Dave ran to the well screaming. His friends were trying to tell him his dog wasn't in the well but he was too worried to listen. He leaned over the well casing yelling for his dog. He thought he was at the bottom of the

well." Harley looked again at Thomas as if seeing his long-a-go child. "Someone or something
spooked my Dave. No one knew what happened. One minute he was there, the next he
was gone."

"What do you mean? Did he fall in the well?"
Thomas asked, "And, the dog and Mick, what
about them?"

"The black demon wasn't in the well. He had
jumped plumb over it chasing the stick with
Mick hot on his trail," Harley said.

"Booger heard Dave scream as he fell in the
well. The dog grabbed the stick, circled Mick,
and made for the well," Grandpa said in a voice
that sounded like a small boy's.

"The dog jumped up on the wall surrounding the well and begin to howl an ungodly
noise. Mick ran for the dog. I think he would
have pushed him in but . . . " Harley said.

"What?" Thomas felt the terrible pain of the
old man but the excitement of the strange tale
held him in its grip. He had to know what happened. "Grandpa, what—?"

"Booger turned on Mick! He grabbed him
like a rag doll, ripping, and shaking, until Mick
was bleeding everywhere. Then Mick was down
and Booger was at his throat." Grandpa pulled
a handkerchief and honked into it.

Tears ran down Harley's wrinkled face. "I
was the one with the stick then. I beat Booger
within the inch of his life but still he held on to
Mick."

"With a voice that sounded like Dave's, you
yelled, 'Fetch!' Then, Harley, you threw your

stick!" Grandpa was staring into space as though seeing the scene replayed. "And the dog let go and ran!"

"Mick ran, too. I'll never know how he got up and raced off after the dog but rage is a strange bed-fellow," Harley said.

"What happened to them?"

"No one knows. In the distance we could hear Mick's screams of fury and Booger's yelps and snarls." Harley pointed toward the back of his property. "An old cemetery adjoins my place at the back. It sits on a hill. Farther on the land drops off into the river. We could tell they'd headed that way by their noise. Then it was like they vanished off the face of the earth. Neither of them ever came back. "

"What about Dave?"

As though drawn by an invisible string, Harley started toward the barn. Tom and Thomas dogged his footsteps. "We hunted that well for days. Men would go down and come back, go down and come back, always empty handed. Finally, they gave up. Dave was gone, too."

Thomas trudged after Grandpa and Harley knowing any minute they'd turn and say, "Boo!" and laugh at him for believing the wild tale. He chuckled, thinking how he'd tell them they hadn't fooled him!

Chapter 4

Dave, Mick, and Booger

Thomas's thoughts slowed his steps. Now, he hurried to catch up thinking, *It's one of the best ghost stories I've ever heard.* He couldn't wait to tell Lefty.

Grandpa and Harley kept moving with grim determination. Then, it dawned on Thomas with bloodcurdling clarity. The horrible story he'd just heard was true! The old man's boys were missing or dead and his grandpa had been there. Jeez! Young Tom had been a part of it. How could a boy ever forget a terrible thing like that?

Harley's excursion skirted the barn. They stood before the casement of a boarded-up well which stood like a shrine to the long ago tragedy.

The wood on one side of the well had been chiseled out with just enough room to fit a picture frame.

Thomas leaned down and wiped off the heavy glass that protected a picture of a younger Harley, a pretty young woman, two boys and a black dog. Beneath it was written these words.

Near Branson, Missouri
On a hilly, curvy, road,

Lived a donkey, a pig,
And an old horny toad.
It was beautiful country
With no one around.
So they raised their voices
In a joyful sound.
Oink, oink, croak, hee-haw.

"Ma used to sing that ditty to the boys when they were babies. When she got to the last line they'd join in, 'Oink, oink, croak, hee-haw.' Of course the boys outgrew the song. But Ma still hummed it around the house. Sometimes, if one of them came in feeling playful and she was humming that song, they sneak up behind her and whisper, 'Oink, oink, croak, hee-haw.' Then they'd give her a big kiss on the cheek. It was kind of a watchword of their very own."

Harley wiped at his eyes and continued, "Ma grieved herself to death. She didn't last more than a year after the boys left. I just stayed here farming. Sometimes late at night I think I hear my boys and that dog out near the barn. Now and then I walk down here hoping for . . . I don't know what."

He leaned down and ran a gnarled finger over the glass. "One day I got the idea to make the well a keystone." Harley's voice quavered, "Oink, oink, croak, hee-haw."

"Harley, I can't tell you how sorry I am to have brought back all these memories," Grandpa said, as he and Thomas followed Harley to the barn.

Harley opened the barn door and went

inside. He flipped a switch flooding the old barn with light. The outside of the barn might looked old but inside—

"It's just like yesterday!" Grandpa gasped. "Only better!"

"This barn is a promise to myself that one day my boys might come home. I know it's foolish thinking, but it kept my hands and mind busy all these years."

Thomas walked across the gleaming hardwood floor toward a basketball which lay beneath a state-of-the-art backboard. He whistled in admiration as he picked up the ball, hefted it for weight, and began to dribble. Bounce-bounce.

Harley watched dreamily, his head tilted to one side as if his thoughts merged with the sound.

"Swish!" Thomas's shot ripped the net for a clean basket.

"Thomas, maybe—" Grandpa began.

"Leave the boy alone, Tom. That's what this place needs, a boy to break it in. Toss it here, boy." Harley held out fragile hands cupped to catch the ball.

Thomas tossed the ball to him, wincing to think of the pain he might be causing the frail fingers.

Quick as a flash, Harley dribbled to the side, let go a jump shot which slipped through the net without even a swish.

"Wow!" Thomas gulped.

"Looks like someone has been practicing." Grandpa grinned.

"If them boys of mine should come back I need to be ready." Harley's eyes shone with a glimmer of hope. "Meantime, I've got someone to practice with . . . for awhile."

Thomas tossed the ball he'd rebounded with more force this time. "You sure have, Mister Jones."

"Just call me Harley, son."

Thomas looked at his grandpa, who nodded.

"Tom, sometimes it does a mind good to clear out the cobwebs," Harley said. "Those days we just remembered are the old town of Branson with trees for miles, hills and hollers, and places to get lost." He hesitated. "Wells that don't give up their dead."

"I know. I remember old Branson and its haunts."

"Life passed me by as I sat grieving for my wife and waiting for my boys to come back." A shadow passed over the old man's features. "Then last spring you visited and asked to rent my field to sell fireworks. It was like a sign from the past. Get on with it, old man, I told myself."

"Thanks, Harley. Maybe it is time for you to get a life."

"And, then I thought about people coming on to my land. The land that swallowed up my sons and Booger. The land that killed my wife. And I wished I could take back my promise to you."

Grandpa looked at Thomas with a pleading question in his eyes.

Thomas walked to the old man and handed the basketball to him. "Mister Jones, er,

Harley, I'm sorry for your troubles. I really want to sell fireworks on your land. But if you don't want us to be here, then, me and Grandpa won't hold you to your promise." It seemed like an omen as he said the words. Like, selling fireworks here had been too good to be true. It wasn't meant to happen anyway.

As Harley took the basketball he held on to Thomas's hand. He looked deep into his eyes as he issued orders, "Boy, you've got chores to do. What are you standing there for? Get on down to the field and get started."

Thomas shrank from this old man who almost seemed a figment of his imagination. He tried to pull his hand away.

But Harley held on tight. "Don't think I'm crazy, son. It just feels good to have a young boy's hand in mine again. I gave my word and I'm sticking to it." He cackled, "I might even shoot a few of them firecrackers myself."

"Er, we've got a rule, we don't shoot fireworks when we're selling. Just before and after," Thomas, ever the good manager, promised.

"Good rule, boy! See that you stick to it." Harley started out the barn door, then turned, and tossed the ball to Thomas. "You got any rules about shooting basketballs?"

"No sir, Harley!" Thomas gulped.

"Then, you and I have a date to play HORSE," Harley said as the door slammed behind him.

"Let's get down to the field and get our chores started," Grandpa muttered, heading for their fireworks location with Thomas close behind.

Thinking about Harley, Thomas and Grandpa worked in silence. Before they had driven all the stakes in the dry, hard packed earth outlining where the fireworks tent should be set, Thomas knew why TNT and Lefty had laughed when he suggested he and Grandpa set up the tent by themselves.

"What's the matter, your hands sore?" Grandpa eyed the ground and positioned the last stake.

Thomas couldn't keep quiet any longer. "How come you never told me the story of the missing boys?"

"Like I said, I guess I buried that memory as deep as those two boys and that dog are buried somewhere." Grandpa slammed the post maul down on the stake driving it into the earth.

"So you think Dave, Mick, and Booger are dead and buried?"

"Who knows? Now, that memories are dredged up, I recall rumors Bud brought home. Wild and crazy stories about Mick and how he'd been planning on running off and joining up with a bunch of gangsters that last night." Grandpa pulled a handkerchief from his pocket and mopped his forehead, "Let's get this stuff loaded. I'd like to get home before dark."

Thomas watched the slow, steady stream of traffic edge by on the highway as Grandpa tried to find an opening.

"How could those boys just disappear?" Thomas turned to look over his shoulder at the barn in the distance.

"Let it rest." Grandpa waved a 'thank you' to a driver who motioned him to pull in front of him on the highway.

Thomas pulled out the 'haunt' book and read stories that didn't seem so strange after what he'd just heard. The miles flew by and soon they were at the city limits of Springfield.

"Hometown looks pretty good don't you think?"

"Sure," Thomas said but his mind was still back in Branson on the Harley Jones farm where they'd be selling firework in less than two weeks. He whispered, "Oink, oink, croak, hee-haw."

Chapter 5
Freddie

"Every home needs a dog!" Martin said to Thomas as they drove toward the animal shelter.

Thomas heard an echo of his and Wendy's words the past week since they'd returned from the fireworks display. CC had stolen both their hearts.

"I wish Grandpa was with us. He'll be surprised when he finds out we have our own dog." Thomas squirmed with excitement.

Martin nodded.

"Mom didn't want me to have a dog because we'd have to keep him tied up in the city." Thomas thought of the morning spent checking the fence that surrounded their back yard. The new dog house stood near the gate, waiting.

"It won't be long and we'll have all kinds of room for a dog to run." Martin took his eyes from the road long enough to share a smile with Thomas.

"Wow! It'll be cool to live in the country. When are they going to start building our house? You think it'll be finished by the end of the year?"

"I wouldn't call it the country, more like the suburbs. Carol wants to be able to move in before the baby comes. Maybe we can have Thanksgiving dinner there!"

"Great! Hey, there's the animal shelter. Look at all the dogs!" Thomas could hardly wait for Martin to park the car.

Inside, Thomas's gaze scanned the cages of dogs. "Which kind makes a good watchdog?"

"A dog that's not mean. Wendy will want him as a pet. But he'll need to be alert and let us know if strangers come around."

"Maybe a collie, like CC? I could take him with me to sell fireworks."

"That's a good idea! A dog can protect you and Grandpa out there in the country at night."

"Sure, he can watch the tent. Grandpa and I can sleep in his camper. If General hears anything, he'll bark and we can check it out."

"General? You think you can find a collie to fit that name?

"Yep, I'd kind of like our dog to outrank Lefty's. CC's real name is Colonel Charlie. Do you like the name, General?"

"Well, we've got to name our dog something. Let's see if the name fits the dog."

Thomas started to stick his hand through an opening in a cage to pat a big rottweiler. "Hey! He likes me!"

"You, kid! Can't you read the sign?" A tall, thin man strode toward them, pointing toward a large sign, DON'T PET THE ANIMALS. "That rottweiler isn't the friendliest dog around. He could take your arm off."

Thomas stepped back quickly when the dog snarled at the man. As they moved on down the path, Thomas whispered, "I don't think the dog was as mean as the man."

Martin gave him a stern look, "Don't judge a man until you know him. It's his job to make sure people don't get hurt here. Dogs can be fickle around strangers." His face softened. "Don't worry, son, we'll find the right dog. There's one around here just meant for us."

Thomas heard a loud yelping coming from inside a pen farther down the way. He saw the same man slam the gate of the pen and stride off in the opposite direction.

"Come on, Martin. Let's see what kind of a dog can make that noise." Thomas hurried toward the pen.

Huddled in the far corner of the pen inside a dirty, box-like structure was a little terrier. Maybe he was solid white. It was hard to tell because his fur was matted with dirt. He sounded like a baby crying as he barked.

"Did you ever see anything so pitiful?" Thomas hunkered down by the side of the pen where he could get a better look at the little dog. He crooned, "What's the matter, boy?" The dog turned toward his voice.

Black, button eyes stared at Thomas reproachfully from beneath strains of stringy hair. Slowly, the pup edged sideways and slipped through an opening on the cheese-crate-like box. He shook his rangy body and straightened proudly as if he'd achieved some-thing special. Bracing his front paws, he reared his head back and yipped at Thomas.

"You're a spunky one, aren't you, boy?"

"Spunky, maybe, but a General?" Martin's attention wandered across the aisle where a spotted grey and black hound was prancing around his pen. "Let's check out this one. He looks like he might make a good watch dog."

Later, still undecided, they made their way back up the rows of dogs. "I don't think I've ever seen so many dogs. What do you think, Thomas?"

"I know just the one!" Thomas walked quickly back toward the front of the walkway.

"Which—?" Martin watched as Thomas approached the pen that held the grey and black hound.

"So, you like the hound?" Martin paused, as Thomas moved past the hound's pen and stopped in front of the gate where the little white terrier still whimpered softly.

"Here little fellow, come on over and let me see what's the matter." Thomas stuck a finger through the wire.

Slowly the pup stood on long, wiry legs. One ear perked up. His mouth stretched into a thin line beneath his moist, black nose as he studied Thomas quizzically.

"That's right. You're a good boy. Come over and let me have a look at you," Thomas continued to croon softly.

Moving cautiously, the dog limped across the pen. He stopped and sniffed the ground near the gate and yelped.

"Look, Martin, his front paw is bleeding. What do you think is the matter?" Thomas reached into his pocket and brought out some beef jerky. He tore off a little piece and tossed it in front of the pooch.

"I don't think they'll like you feeding the dogs," Martin warned.

"But he looks half starved." Thomas crooned, "Come here pup."

The little dog snatched up the piece of food and swallowed it in one gulp. He moseyed closer to Thomas keeping a watchful eye on his hand which held another piece of meat.

"Want this, boy?" Thomas stuck his hand farther inside the opening. "Then, you'll have to come and get it."

"Yip, yip!" The little dog raced forward, grabbed the meat, and hurried back to safety to eat.

A coarse voice yelled directly behind Thomas. "Hey kid, you hard of hearing?"

Thomas jerked as a hand closed on his shoulder roughly.

Martin turned toward the man. "Get your hand off the boy!"

The thin man quickly removed his hand but jerked open the gate of the terrier's pen and entered. Striding toward the cowering pup, he removed a long stick from his belt and pointed it in the dog's direction.

"Yip, yip!" The little dog ran at the man nipping at his pants leg like an ant attacking an elephant.

"Why you small-time-Freddie-bucking-to-be-a-general!" The man raised the stick as he kicked the dog.

"Hey!" Martin moved forward as the man advanced on the dog.

"Come here," Thomas hesitated only a second over the name, "General" as he held out his arms.

"Yip, yip!" The little bit of fur lunged past the man with the upraised stick, passed Martin, and jumped straight into Thomas's arms.

"Why, you mangy, little . . . spitfire." The tall man's lip curled back in a snarl as he headed toward Thomas.

"You touch him and you answer to me!" Martin hurried toward Thomas.

The man turned abruptly.

Martin almost collided with him.

"I wasn't going to bother your boy. It's the dog that needs to be taught a lesson. I'd advise you folks to move along and pick out a dog that knows how to behave." He reached for the pup who glared at him from the safety of Thomas's arms.

"It's the dog I'm talking about," Martin said in a stern voice, "I believe my son and I have made our choice. This little spitfire is just what we were looking for, don't you think so, Thomas?"

Thomas, smiling ear-to-ear, clutched the rag-a-muffin puppy against him. "Thanks, Martin. Come on General! Let's go home."

"You gentlemen found yourselves a pet?" A lady dressed in fashion overalls called from the office doorway. "Jervis, is there a problem?"

The thin man shot a warning look at Thomas and Martin. "No problem here, Missus Taylor." He smirked. "Boss, looks like we've found a home for this cute little terrier." The man reached a hand toward the dog as if to pat him but withdrew it quickly when the dog curled his lip in a snarl.

Jervis muttered, "Watch it!" Glowering, he turned and strode toward the back of the pound.

Inside, as they finished the paperwork, Daisy Taylor introduced Martin and Thomas to the new manager, Lester Jones, a retired Marine, who had just moved to Springfield from Texas.

Lester turned from the window overlooking the pound. "Tell me, gentlemen, what was your impression of Jervis?"

"Sir, he—" Thomas began.

"Thomas, I'm sure these professionals don't need us to explain their employees to them. Sometimes actions speak louder than words." Martin smiled as he reached to shake Lester's hand.

"Actually, Jervis was here before me, so I can't qualify as his employer yet." Lester smiled at Daisy. "I'm just visiting to get the feel of things until next month when Daisy, er, Missus Taylor, moves up to district manager."

Daisy started to speak just as a tall, red-headed boy, about Thomas's age came through the back door. "Dad, that man . . . he's upsetting the animals again."

"Thanks, son." Lester looked at Daisy, who nodded.

Together, they excused themselves and followed the boy out into the maze of cages.

Thomas hugged General closer as he heard snarls of pain coming from the back. He started toward the door as he heard shouts.

Martin's voice stopped him, "Thomas, let's

leave it to Daisy and Lester to run this shelter. They look perfectly qualified to handle their job."

A few minutes later, the tall, thin man burst into the office. He stomped to a locker where he flung open the door and grabbed a lunch box. Quickly, he pulled open a file cabinet, extracted something, and stuck it into his pocket. As he pulled his hand out, a small bottle fell to the floor rolling toward Thomas. As Jervis moved to retrieve it, General growled from the refuge of Thomas's arms.

"What the—?" Jervis was startled to see Martin, Thomas, and the little terrier, standing at the far side of the room. "I should have known." He clenched his hand into a fist and shook it in their direction. "You'll pay for getting me fired."

"We didn't . . ." Thomas began.

Daisy and Lester strode into the office followed by Lester's son.

Jervis said curtly, "You've got my address. Send me my pay." He darted a mean look at Thomas and stomped out.

Daisy stuck her hands deep into the pockets of her overalls with a embarrassed shrug. "I knew that was coming. He's been so moody lately, and he takes it out on the animals." She smiled nervously. "Lester, I'm glad you were here." She patted the boy's arm, "You, too. Thanks for alerting us to the situation."

Lester turned to Martin and Thomas. "Sorry for the confusion." He drew his son forward. "I'd like to introduce my son. David. This is . . ."

he glanced at their application forms lying on the desk, "Martin Taylor and his son Thomas." Lester grinned at Daisy. "You guys got the same last name, Daisy."

"I noticed that before the ruckus started." She shrugged gracefully.

David moved toward Thomas. The little white terrier's body began to wag with excitement. He licked David's fingers as he reached to pat him. "Found you a new home, have you, Freddie?" He lifted the dog's face and stared into his little, black eyes. "Going to get your freedom in spite of Jervis?"

Jervis's words sprang to Thomas's mind. He muttered them aloud, "Small-time-Freddie-bucking-to-be-a-general."

David nodded. "So, you heard him, too. Jervis tried to keep this dog locked in that dirty box in his cage." A smile broke across the boy's face as the dog barked. "Sure, he couldn't keep you from your freedom, could he, Freddie? You find a way out every time."

Lester moved closer and clapped his son on the shoulder. He addressed his question to the dog. "So, Freddie, what does the future hold for you?"

"General is going to be a watchdog at our fireworks tent," Thomas said proudly.

The little dog straightened up as though he understood.

"Fireworks!" David grinned. "You're selling fireworks? Where is your tent?"

Lester laughed. "David talks fireworks almost as much as dogs. He can hardly wait for the Fourth of July Commemorative next Saturday night at Ozark. They promise quite a fireworks display."

Thomas looked at Martin with a question in his eyes.

Martin smiled a proud-father smile. "Actually, Thomas and his friend Lefty are receiving an award that night."

David's eyes grew round. "You, too?"

Thomas heard, "You two?" He nodded. "Yep, I'm Thomas Scott and my friend, Lefty Tucker—"

David laughed, "No, I meant you—t-double-o?" Suddenly, he stopped, thought for a minute, and his eyes lit up. "I thought your name was Taylor." He looked from Martin to Thomas, "but you," he pointed to Martin, "are the Taylor, and," he pointed to Thomas, "are one of the two boys who knocked out the ter-rorist with baseballs on the way back from Honk Kong! Remember Dad, Pappy DeMouse said—"

Lester clapped his son on the shoulder stop-ping him in mid-sentence. "Slow down, David! Too much excitement will cause—"

This time, it was David who stopped his father. He drew a deep breath, let it out, and said in a calm voice, "It looks like we are all going to be at Ozark next Saturday night. My grandfather is Pappy DeMouse!"

Martin looked dumbfounded.

Thomas emitted a respectful whistle, "Man! Your grandpa is a World War Two Ace? Like the Red Baron?"

Martin stared at Thomas in wonder, as did Lester at his son.

"Pappy DeMouse served in World War Two, of course. He says he got credit for nineteen aces." David watched Thomas for a reaction.

"They credited Red Baron with eighty!"

"But, the Red Baron, Manfred von Richtofen, was German. That was the first World War. Pappy DeMouse says those crates were put together with chicken wire and you should have been able to pick them off easily. My grandfather, First Lieutenant 'Pappy' DeMouse, is being honored on Saturday night because he is a hero and a native son of the Ozarks—"

Lester once more clamped a hand on his son's shoulder stopping him in mid-sentence. "David, I'm sure you boys could discuss the merits of Aces all day. But, I must warn you, once more, excitement is not the right medicine for your—"

David's face flushed the color of the thatch of hair that curled tightly to his head. "I'm sorry." He smiled as the color receded back into his hairline. "I guess my grandpa's career is an inspiration to me."

"As well it should be," Martin said, slipping smoothly into the conversation. He looked at Thomas. "My son surprises me every day with a bit of inspiration. How did you know?"

Thomas grinned. "Lefty told me. TNT is going to compare those Aces to WONDERMAN when she introduces the fireworks display Saturday night to sort of tie the theme together. Like protecting the skies, and all."

This time Lester and David were speechless.

Martin held up his hands as if saying let's back up a minute. "Remember, we started this conversation with fireworks?"

They nodded.

"My son and his grandpa Scott are going to be running a tent in Branson for TNT, the lady who owns Rainbow Fireworks. She will be supplying the fireworks for the show Saturday night at Ozark." He paused, seeing comprehension dawning in both their eyes. "When Thomas and his grandpa accompanied TNT and her grandson, Lefty, to Honk Kong on a fireworks buying trip, she submitted designs for fireworks shells that are named after the boys. WONDERMAN is named for Thomas's imaginary super-hero."

Thomas nodded with a big grin.

"SLIDER is named for Lefty's talent with a baseball. You'll see both shells shot off Saturday night as a part of the display."

"So, the Hong Kong trip was where Thomas and Lefty beaned the terrorist!" David nodded in awe.

"Where is your tent?" Lester asked. "I guess we'll have to visit."

"On old Mister Jones's farm at Branson."

The sound of squealing tires from the front of the building interrupted their conversation. Everyone moved to a window as an old, green pickup with a smashed tail-gate ripped out of the pound and onto the street.

"Looks like Jervis has left the building."

Daisy had been listening to the conversation with interest. Now, she tried for humor with a remembered exit line from Elvis.

Martin chuckled. "Thomas, I think we've taken up enough of these good people's time. General Freddie, here, is ready for his freedom."

Daisy held up some tickets. "I was going to offer you some complimentary tickets for the concert Saturday night since the musical groups, Alabama and the Ozark Mountain Daredevils, are putting on the show in support of the animal shelter." She stuck the tickets in her overall pockets, "I guess you and your family will be sitting front and center in the honor section as will the family of First Lieutenant Pappy DeMouse." She indicated Lester and David.

"If you need any help selling fireworks, my dad and I are available." David offered, looking at his dad for confirmation.

Lester's manner grew distant. "David, I think Mr. Taylor is right. We all have things to do and places to go. We better let these new dog owners get on their way."

"But, Dad, it's like an opportunity of a lifetime. Didn't you hear—" David pleaded.

"David, Thomas and his grandpa will probably have all kinds of business on the Jones farm. There's a lot of traffic on that road nowadays. But, you seem to be forgetting. You don't hire yourself. The boss does the hiring. Let these gentlemen be on their way. Branson is a ways down the road."

Martin gently moved Thomas a little closer to the door. "Actually, we live here in Springfield." He took out a business card and handed it to Lester Jones. "If you ever need a good detective agency, just call me. But, even a good detective could get confused with all these same last names floating around."

Laughter followed as the group tried to sort out last names that had been mentioned.

Lester took the card Martin offered. "Well, you never know who and what you'll be needing, right? Especially if one wants to keep up with the Taylors and the Joneses." Lester grinned at Daisy letting her know he could use cliques, too.

While the grownups were talking, Thomas and David had their heads together chatting a mile a minute. As they started to leave, Thomas stuck a piece of paper in his pocket and promised,

"I'll call you. Maybe your dad will let you come and play basketball."

Lester started to put a hand on his son's shoulder but David moved away. "Only practice, Dad, not play. I know what I can do and what I can't. Besides, I can do a follow-up on General Freddie."

The little dog wagged its body against Thomas. As they moved forward, Thomas's foot struck a bottle on the floor. It spun across the room.

David picked it up. "Someone lost their medicine." He turned the bottle and read from the label, "Alpsorax."

Lester reached for the bottle. "Let me see. That's an anti–depressant drug." He looked at Daisy. "Do you know—"

"That's the bottle that fell from Jervis's pocket when he got something out of that file cabinet," Thomas said.

"Jervis took something from the file cabinet?" Daisy opened the door to look. "Nothing seems to be missing unless. . ." She fingered a bunch of keys. "I'm not sure how many keys were here."

"Did Jervis have a key to the shelter?" Lester asked.

"No."

"You said he had been moody?" Lester asked.

"More so, the last few weeks. That's when he started being abusive to the animals. Some of the other employees were afraid to be here alone with him."

Lester turned the bottle around in his fingers examining it. "I'll do a little research on this medicine."

Martin moved toward the exit with Thomas following holding the terrier. "Remember, if you need my services, just call."

Martin agreed to let Thomas ride in the back seat with General Freddie to give the little dog an early chance at freedom in the floorboard.

Thomas was already playing with his new friend as Martin pulled onto the highway. He missed seeing an old green pickup pull out of a side street and into the traffic behind them.

But, Martin, ever the detective, kept the

pickup in sight through his rear-view mirror noting the license plates for later reference.

"Why are you stopping again?" Thomas asked, after Martin had made several unscheduled stops in different parts of town.

"Checking out things," Martin said in an off-hand manner.

Finally, Martin headed home after assuring himself he had lost the green pickup.

Chapter 6
Grandpa's Research

"Look at his two little brown ears!" Wendy traced a soapy finger over General Freddie's ear, sculpting it to his head. She let go and immediately the ear sprang back to attention. She giggled as the pup stared up at her.

The little terrier tried to squirm out of Thomas's grasp as Martin rubbed soft lather all over the dog.

"He looks like a pirate with that brown patch over one eye." Thomas carefully wiped the dog's face.

"He's so cute! But he looks too timid to be named General. Let's call him Spot or Curly or Whitey." Wendy rattled off names as she picked up the pup's sore foot and examined it.

A soft, low growl started in the dog's stomach and moved up his throat.

"Watch out!" Thomas saw the dog's jaws open and snap at Wendy's finger.

"Ouch!" Wendy cried, as she tried to remove her finger from the dog's mouth.

"Wendy!" Martin moved toward his daughter.

Thomas continued to soothe the dog with soft words.

Wendy began to giggle as she worked her finger from the dog's mouth. "Don't worry, Dad! He didn't hurt me. He just wanted me to leave his sore foot alone. All he did was nibble on my finger and say, 'GFF!'" She held out her finger as proof.

"I could just see that little spitfire with your finger dangling from his mouth!" Martin sank down beside the tub. "He didn't even break the skin. But he's not timid. I think General is a perfect name for you, little fella."

"Don't worry, Martin. General Freddie's papers said he's had all his shots." Thomas paused. "Wendy, what did you say the dog said?"

Wendy patted the dog's head, and giggled. "GFF!"

"That's it! That's what we'll call him. General Freddie Freedom—GFF! You know like CC is Corporal Charlie."

"Well, GFF, the vet can fix your paw," Wendy said. "You're going to have to get well fast if you're going to guard the fireworks tent for Grandpa, Thomas, and me."

"What do you think, GFF? Can you handle the job?" Thomas lifted the dog out of the tub and engulfed him in a fluffy towel.

A flurry of white jumped from Thomas's grasp and stood before them looking smaller with his wet fur plastered against his tiny frame. Suddenly, he arched his back and began to shake water everywhere.

"Where'd you get that drowned rat?" Grandpa stood in the garage door staring at them.

"Grandpa! Where have you been all week?" Thomas snatched up the pup and walked over to him.

"Doing a little research. What's this you got?"

"GFF's our new watchdog."

"Humpppp! Watchdog? Where's the rest of him? It looks like something Booger might have chewed up and spit out."

Grandpa's mention of Dave's and Mick's long ago dog surprised Thomas until a thought occurred to him, "I bet you've been researching the lost boys and their dog."

Grandpa nodded.

"What lost boys? Who's Booger?" Wendy demanded. Without waiting for an answer she continued, "And, don't talk about GFF that way, he's so cuteeee!"

"GFF? What kind of a name is that?" Grandpa asked. "Sounds like you're talking dog talk."

The pup struggled loose from Thomas's grip, jumped to the floor, and ran to Grandpa. He yipped as he circled Grandpa's legs. His little pink tongue flickered inside his mouth like laughter trying to escape.

"Looks like he approves of you, Grandpa." Wendy giggled.

"He probably thinks Grandpa's bark is worse than his bite."

Thomas grinned.

"Let's go show Carol how good he looks after his bath," Martin suggested, "And, Tom, why don't you tell us more about the dog you called Booger and the lost boys."

Thomas lay stretched out on the rug with GFF, whose fur looked bleached white. Wendy lay beside them but soon crawled onto the couch and snuggled between her dad and Carol as Grandpa spun his tale.

"And Mick chased Booger into the woods and through the cemetery at the back of the Jones property," Grandpa finished.

"Did Dave really drown in the well?" Wendy's voice sounded scared.

"Honey, they think so but they never found his, er—"

Carol cleared her throat cutting off Tom's last words. "That's the strangest story I ever heard, Tom. You ought to phone it in to Unsolved Mysteries."

Martin nodded. "So, they never found either of the Jones boys or their dog, Booger?"

"I should have known a private investigator would get right to the heart of the story," Grandpa said, nodding at Martin.

"If you think that's strange. Listen to this!" Thomas buried his fingers in GFF's fur. "Grandpa said he had completely forgot about the missing boys until we talked to Mister Jones."

Martin mused, "It's not unusual for people, especially kids, to block unpleasant memories from their mind." He turned to Tom, "Didn't they report the boys missing?"

"Yes, but you've got to remember when I was a kid, back in the late thirties and early forties, the world was a different place. Especially in the back woods of Branson."

"Even so, Tom—" Martin started.

"Grandpa's right, Martin," Thomas assured

him. "I emailed Ahunk, Sydney Snyder, the whole story. He reminded me they didn't communicate like we do today. There were no cell phones, no television—"

Wendy groaned. "No television?"

Thomas nodded. "Sydney said people listened to radios."

Grandpa chuckled. "If you were lucky enough to have one. If we could scrape together enough money to go to a movie, we could watch newsreels of gangsters. They were almost as good as the main feature."

"Grandpa, Sydney and I were talking about that. Didn't you say Uncle Bud told you something about Mick running off with gangsters?" Thomas reminded him.

"Funny, you'd ask," Grandpa said. "I called Bud after we got home last week and told him about you, Harley, and me. He remembered more about the missing boys and their dog than I did. That's what started my research."

GFF stirred. He emitted a soft noise that resembled his name.

"What's wrong, boy?" Thomas pulled the dog against him.

Grandpa rubbed his chin, and began, "When I was a boy, I tagged after Bud and Dave Jones. They hung around gas stations just to see what kind of automobiles drove in to fuel up."

Thomas moved to an upright position and rested his back against a chair near the front window where the last rays of light were beginning to fade. GFF moved restlessly, eyeing the window. Then he jumped on Thomas's lap and snuggled down.

Grandpa continued, "Or, you could hang around and hear the old men talk about John Dillinger, Baby Face Nelson, Machine Gun Kelly, Bonnie and Clyde, and Ma Barker."

Wendy sat upright. "I saw the movie about Bonnie and Clyde. They robbed banks but they wrote poems, too."

Thomas nodded. "So, they drove old cars like Bonnie and Clyde?"

"Or Robert Redford in "The Great Gatsy?" Carol reminded them.

"You've got the picture." Grandpa nodded. "Cars changed the world and made it smaller. But, cars broke down and that's where Mick came in."

"I thought Mick was a kid," Thomas said.

"Mick was older than his brother Dave, who was about Bud's age. But Mick was a born mechanic. And, in those days a good mechanic was worth his weight in gold."

"And that made him important to anyone who owned a car," Martin broke in.

"That's right! Bud, Dave, and Mick watched other mechanics take engines apart and repair them. Bud and Dave never got the hang of it but Mick did. He became known as one of the best automobile mechanics in the area."

"Was that why the gangsters wanted Mick to run away with them, Grandpa? To fix their cars?" Thomas's eyes were wide with excitement.

Grandpa nodded.

"This must have been in the early forties." Martin had been following the story closely. "I thought most of the big gangsters were gone by nineteen thirty-four."

Tom nodded. "You're probably right. But ever once in awhile a strange car with a city dude would show up at the garage looking for the kid mechanic. Mick made a lot of extra money fixing cars."

"Branson was just a no name spot in the road in those days, wasn't it, Tom?" Carol asked.

"Yes, but cars had to have gas and stations brought people to town. Bud told me there were rumors going around that Mick had been asked to join up with a gang. He didn't know they were part of a ring that stole cars and passed them down the line all through Joplin, down through Texas, up through Frederick, Oklahoma, and out to California."

GFF pushed off Thomas's lap, stretched his long legs, and moved stiffly toward the couch where Wendy was sitting. Half way there fatigue overtook him and he slumped against Grandpa's chair.

"So, Bud thought Mick was planning on running away that night?" Martin asked.

"Grandpa! Remember, Mister Jones said Mick was never on time for supper. But that night he was there early and seemed to be in a hurry?" Thomas said.

"You're right!" Grandpa nodded. "That could have been the reason. He was going to meet the gangsters that night."

Suddenly, GFF leaped up, barked his shrill little yips and raced toward the window. Jumping up, he placed his paws on the low window sill, plastered his nose against the window, and began growling.

Thomas was up and after him. "What is it, GFF? Is something out there?"

"Get away from the window, Thomas!" Martin was right behind Thomas peering into the dusk. Outside the mercury street lights were beginning to flicker before becoming fully illuminated.

"The dog probably needs to take a walk outside," Grandpa suggested.

"You mean? The bathroom?" Thomas jerked the dog up abruptly, "Don't you dare, GFF! I promised Mom you were house broke."

"Yanking him up like that could help things along. Come on, Thomas. Let's you, Martin, and I take the dog out for his evening constitutional. I need to get started home anyway." Grandpa headed toward the door.

"But, what if GFF is right? What if something or someone was out there?" Wendy shrank deeper into the couch near Carol.

"Honey, there's nothing out there. Come over here. I'll show you." Martin motioned for his daughter.

"No thanks, Dad. I'm already going to have a hard enough time sleeping tonight." Wendy moaned.

"Sorry Wendy, I shouldn't have told a story like that in front of a little girl. I didn't realize you would get scared."

Wendy laughed, "I'm not scared. I just can't rest until this mystery is solved."

"Come on, Wendy. Let's pop some corn. We can watch a movie when the guys get back from walking the dog." Carol pulled Wendy with her into the kitchen.

Thomas started toward the front door.

"Wait!" Martin's gruff voice stopped him in his tracks.

GFF growled low in his throat.

Grandpa looked at Martin with a question in his eyes.

Martin motioned them back. He crossed to the door, eased it open, and glanced outside as the squeal of tires burned rubber near the curb down the street.

Thomas, clutching GFF, ran with Grandpa to the window in time to see an old green pick-up careen around the corner on two wheels.

"Martin! Wasn't that—"

Glancing toward the kitchen, Martin put a warning finger to his lips and slowly nodded his head.

Chapter 7
The Party

"Stop that ball, guys!"

Thomas stuck out his sneaker, snared the run-a-way basketball and flicked his toe upward. The ball raced up his leg. He caught it and tossed it back to a tall, slim, kid in a over-sized T-shirt, jeans, and a ball cap on back-wards. "Hey Jo-Jo!" He grinned.

"Hey, Thomas." Flashing a pretty-boy smile, the kid nodded toward the back yard where the artillery shell box with WONDERMAN and a bundle of five/four hundred ZEUS firecrackers were being used as a Fourth of July centerpiece for the Friday night buffet table. "WONDER-MAN is your fireworks label, right?"

"Sure as shooting!" Thomas beamed.

"Speaking of which, are we going to shoot it tonight?"

"Nope, we'd get in big trouble if we shot fire-works inside the city. But TNT's crew are going to light up WONDERMAN and SLIDER, during the display at Duck's stadium tomorrow night!"

"Hey Jo-Jo, you gonna play ball or talk?" One of the boys on the other team hollered.

"Play!" The kid tossed the basketball effort-lessly through the hoop for three points and moved to play defense.

"Cool move! That guy's good!" David Jones said as he stood near the edge of the basketball court in Thomas's side yard watching kids scrimmage.

Thomas grinned. "Er, David, about that guy
. . ." Thomas broke off as another group of people arrived with food and a pop cooler. Thomas
turned to greet them. Out of the corner of his
eye, he thought he saw a flash of green as a
pickup edged between two SUVs down the
block.

"Jervis wouldn't show up with a crowd
here." Thomas scanned the area where groups
of parents, neighbors, and friends, were visiting on the porch and around the side yard. In
the back yard the grill was going and the buffet table was filled with food.

Lester Jones, who projected the image of a
Marine even in civilian clothes, was engrossed
in conversation with Martin. After the green
pickup incident the other night, Martin had
called the animal shelter to get Jervis's
address. He wanted to check it against the
information he got when he ran the license
plates on Jervis's pickup.

David's voice broke into Thomas's thoughts,
"What was it you were going to say about that
basketball player?"

"Never mind, you'll find out soon enough."
Thomas grinned as he saw the puzzled look on
David's face. "Hey, I'm glad you and your dad
were able to be here tonight. Too bad Pappy
DeMouse didn't get to come. We were all looking forward to meeting him, especially my
grandpa Scott."

David shrugged. "Pappy's resting up for
tomorrow night. He won't admit it but I know
he's excited to be honored with a Commemora-

tive Award. He said he'd meet the boy heros at the ceremony." David's voice echoed sarcasm when he pronounced, boy heroes.

"Boy heroes? He actually called us that?" Thomas wrinkled his nose repeating the phrase the same way David had said it.

"Uh, yeah, you'd have to know my grandpa to understand how he feels about 'this generation of kids who've had the world handed to them on a silver platter.'" He gave Thomas a sheepish smile.

"No sweat, he and Grandpa Scott have a lot in common." Thomas did a gruff imitation of his grandpa, "Thomas, work will make a MAN of you. You kids have it too easy today. Why, back in my day—" Thomas stopped short and swung around as a hand clapped him on the shoulder. "Sorry—"

"Don't mention it, son," Grandpa Scott's voice held a mixture of suppressed laughter and reprimand. "Why don't you introduce me?"

Thomas gulped. "Sure! Grandpa Scott, this is David Jones, Pappy DeMouse's grandson."

David's face merged with his hair color as he extended his hand. His voice had the clipped authority of a military child, "Pleased to meet you, sir. Thomas speaks well of you."

Grandpa grinned at their discomfort. "Yeah, I overheard." Grandpa hesitated giving them time to squirm. Then he put a friendly arm across each of their shoulders. "Don't worry about it. I was young once, too."

In a nearby hammock Wendy and her friend Thayla Hart from down the street were fussing over GFF. The dog was sporting a new collar with an American flag on it in honor of his freedom, Independence Day, and being chosen poster dog for The National Animal Shelter Foundation. Thomas and his family had been delighted when they learned David and Lester had entered a picture of the pup in the competition and he had won.

Richard King, the picture of health after his near death experience with the blood disease, Consanguine, was running around the hammock teasing the girls.

The ball game came to a sweaty halt. The tall, thin, kid in the ball cap nodded at Grandpa and dribbled the ball over to Thomas. "Hey, Stud, we won! I guess that means your team plays ours for champs. Who's your friend?"

David flushed and stuck out his hand. "I'm David Jones. I've been admiring your form. Your long shot is . . . WOW!"

The kid swiped a sweaty hand backside and snatched off the ball cap. Long, brown, hair covered her shoulders. She shook David's hand. "Hi, I'm Jodie! Sometimes my friends call me Jo-Jo. Glad to meet you, David. You play basketball?"

Wendy and Thayla, Jodie's sister, had deserted the hammock and strolled toward the group in time to hear David's stuttered reply, "You're a girl!"

Wendy and Thayla broke into giggles. Wendy said, "Don't feel bad, David. She fooled Thomas first time he met her, too."

Thomas gave Wendy a brotherly shove while grabbing GFF. "Actually, I knew all along . . . "

"Sure Thomas . . . " a chorus of voices teased him.

"You gonna clown around all night or do we play for champs without you?" Deke, one of Thomas's friends called.

Lex, and Jodie, formed a team with Thomas's AAU basketball team mates, Walt and Zeper.

Deke's sister, Fallon, and Thomas's classmate, six foot, six, Kenneth King, who stood palming the basketball, mingled with the rest of their team, while they waited for Thomas to join them.

From the back yard, Martin's voice called, "Come and get it!"

Most of the crowd moved toward the back yard but action was still hot and heavy on the basketball court. The championship depended on the next basket scored. Kids stood in clusters yelling for their favorite players.

Wendy yelled, "GFF is cheering for you, Thomas!" As if on cue, the little terrier started yipping. He broke loose from Wendy's arms and bounded down the sidewalk with Wendy and Thayla in hot pursuit.

Kenneth tossed the ball to Thomas for an outside shot. As the ball swished the net, Wendy's screams, joined by Thayla's cries, and GFF's loud barking came from down the block.

Thomas bounded toward the sounds of distress. David was a few steps behind him and the rest of the players and watchers followed.

Martin emerged from the back yard followed by the crowd of party guests.

A short way down the street, parked near the curb, was Jervis's green pickup. Standing guard was a rottweiler. A chain attached to the huge dog's collar extended over the edge of the pickup bed allowing the dog to move along the side of the vehicle.

Standing just out of reach of the rottweiler was GFF, feet planted, and yipping furiously. Each time the rottweiler moved to intercept GFF, the little dog moved beneath the pickup only to emerge in another spot.

Wendy stayed near the back bumper of the pickup. Thayla was near the front bumper. Each girl was trying to coach GFF to come to them. If they got too near, the rottweiler would lunge at them and they would scream.

The throng of people came to a halt giving the rottweiler plenty of space. Martin scooped up his daughter and carried her away from the pickup. Jodie grabbed her sister's hand and pulled her away. Wendy and Thayla continued to cry as GFF persisted in his adventure with the rottweiler.

"Spartan! Stand!" David shouted the command and the rottweiler froze. "In the pickup, Spartan!" David ordered. Immediately the dog raced to the damaged tail gate and bounded over into the bed of the pickup. "Now, stay!" David's voice softened, "Good Dog!" The rottweiler's tongue lolled to one side of his grinning mouth while his whole body shook with pleasure. He planted himself near the back window of the cab of the pickup.

Thomas stood beside David, his mouth agape with admiration.

"How'd you know the dog's name? Where'd you learn to do that?"

David face was flushed. "Elementary, my dear Watson. I started a training school at the animal shelter. Spartan was one of the first dogs I trained before he disappeared."

"Disappeared? You mean. . .?" A glint of suspicion crept into Thomas's eyes as he looked at the rottweiler and the pickup to which he was chained.

David lifted his eyebrows in a 'who knows' expression but nodded in agreement.

"GFF! Come here!" Thomas demanded as the little dog stayed his ground beneath the pickup barking.

"Freddie! Halt!" David commanded.

GFF stopped barking.

"Freddie! Come!" David shouted.

GFF crawled from under the pickup and ran to David. He looked from Thomas to David and back. Then bounded at Thomas, who opened his arms and caught him close in a hug.

"Man, you're going to have to teach me this training stuff. But why did GFF come to me instead of you?"

"Transferral of—" David began just as his dad emerged from the crowd and came to his side.

"David! You promised you'd take it easy! Look at you!" Lester turned the back of his hand and placed it against his son's forehead.

"You're hot! Come on, I'm taking you home!"

Lester moved forward, obviously expecting the troops to fall in behind him.

"Dad! I'm fine! Just because I had mono last year doesn't mean I have to be a monk the rest of my life!" David said in the same voice he'd used to control the dogs a few minutes before.

Lester pivoted.

Ya-room! The sound reverberated through the residential area of the city followed by an explosion high in the sky.

Heads turned to watch the action as fireballs soared into the heavens. Millions of lights swirled, forming the giant outline of a super hero.

Thomas shouted, "It's WONDERMAN!"

The crowd cheered as another fireball exploded in front of WONDERMAN and became an opponent with weapon raised.

Bolts of fire erupted from WONDERMAN's extended arm flashing across space to eliminate the enemy, who cascaded downward in bursts of color just as sirens began to wail nearby.

Jodi yelled, "I thought you weren't going to shoot WONDERMAN tonight, Thomas!"

"We weren't!" Thomas shouted as he ran. The group followed. "Let's get to the yard and see what happened."

Carol was standing in the side yard with tears streaming down her face as Thomas, Martin, Grandpa, and the guests arrived. Martin lifted her into his arms while others murmured concern that she was having trouble with the baby she was expecting. Thomas walked beside Martin holding his mom's hand.

When Martin started to go into the house, Carol cried harder and pointed to the back yard. "Please, look!" She bawled.

Martin walked to the back yard with the group surrounding him as the image of WONDERMAN rocketed higher in the sky. It exploded into the outline of a spaceship which soared upward and disappeared.

Gasps and exclamations escaped the guests as they viewed the back yard. "The party! What happened?"

The buffet table was tipped on its side. Food was spilled over the ground. The grill toppled on the cement patio in burning disarray. Nearby lay the WONDERMAN artillery shell box. It was empty. Even the launching tube was gone.

Thomas knew without looking that the bundle of five/four hundred ZEUS firecrackers his mom had used for her centerpiece was missing, too.

"All right! Who's in charge here?" Rough voices yelled from the side yard.

The crowd turned as one and stared at police officers standing near the entrance to the back yard. The sound of sirens blared from patrol cars parked in the side yard of the Taylor/Scott residence. The firework fanfare plus the glare of colored lights revolving on top of the patrol cars was drawing a crowd in the streets.

Martin started forward still carrying his

wife. "What's the problem, officers?"

They held their ground surveying the destruction. One officer walked toward a discarded punk, still smoldering. He picked it up and said, "You tell me! Just what's been going on here? You realize it's against the law to shoot fireworks in the city limits, don't you?"

Chapter 8

Commerative Celebration

"You mean someone sneaked in your back yard while you and your friends were watching a dog fight and lit off WONDERMAN?" Lefty Tucker stood with Thomas in the dressing room of the Ducks, a professional baseball team, with a stadium in Ozark, Missouri.

"That about sums it up." Thomas had just finished filling in the details of the evening before.

As honored guests, they were waiting to be escorted to the bandstand, where the musical group, Ozark Mountain Daredevils, was playing. The celebrated quartet, Alabama, would be in concert later. The commemorative awards and the fireworks display would signal an early kick-off of the Fourth of July season.

"What did your mom do when she saw someone lighting the shell?" Lefty asked.

"Mom said she had been in the house getting ready to bring out some more food, so she didn't hear Wendy and Thayla screaming. When she came out the patio door, she couldn't believe the back yard was so quiet and deserted. Then she saw the first glow from the shell. Someone was hovering over it." Running a finger beneath the collar of his white shirt Thomas tried to loosen the knot on his red, white, and blue tie. He shrugged his shoulders to accustom himself to the light weight navy blazer his mom had bought for this special occasion.

"Did she yell?"

Thomas paused to consider. "She said she heard two voices, a man and a boy. The man was yelling at the boy to hurry and light the shell."

"Did she see them?"

"No, they had torn down the patio lights and it was dark. She heard a loud crash and saw the grill fall. The buffet table was on its side with food everywhere."

"And, she was out there by herself with those weirdos?"

"Yes! That's when she screamed," Thomas said.

"I bet they scrambled then."

"She said she heard a man's voice holler for the kid to come on. Just then the shell erupted and burst in the air. She automatically looked up. When she looked back they were gone."

"How did the cops get there so fast?"

"They said they received a nine-one-one call which gave our address. A man's voice said there was a big party going on causing a disturbance. The officers saw the first fireworks explode when they pulled onto the block."

"So, you think it was the guy—what was his name—Jervis? The one who was mean to the animals at the animal shelter?"

"Yeah, he said he'd get even. He thought it was our fault that he got fired. Some kid must have been with him. Martin thinks that kook's been watching our house. He believes it was Jervis looking in our window the other night."

"Why didn't you tell the officers about his pickup with the dog that David said was stolen from the shelter."

"We did! But, when we showed them where the pickup had been parked, it was gone."

"All kind of witnesses saw the pickup parked there, didn't they?"

"Sure, but everyone had left 'cause the party was ruined."

"Didn't Martin get Jervis's home address? Couldn't they check it out?" Lefty persisted.

"When they questioned him, the police officer told Martin Jervis laughed at them. He said his pickup was parked there because he and his son had been walking their dogs. They had three dogs. They left one in the pickup. It was tied up so it couldn't bother anyone."

"Likely story!" Lefty hooted.

Thomas's eyes flashed, "Get this! Jervis said when they got back from walking their dogs some people in that area told him there had been some girls with a little dog pestering his rottweiler. He claimed he might press charges against the girls and have the little dog impounded."

"Man! He sounds like a mean one! I wouldn't want to meet him in a dark alley."

"You talking about me?" The older man stood slim and erect in a uniform that was straight out of a World War II movie. It was covered with medallions, ribbons, and decorative patches.

Thomas and Lefty stared, unable to speak.

"Cat got your tongues? Surely you two can't be the boy heroes? I figured you'd be a mixture of FBI agents, Elliot Ness and Melvin Purvis."

"Pappy DeMouse!" The boys exclaimed in unison.

While the three heroes waited to be presented to the audience in the grandstand, they exchanged stories about past events in their lives and what caused them to be here receiving awards.

"I can't believe you actually met Elliot Ness." Lefty was fascinated with DeMouse's mention of Ness, Purvis, and gangsters like Pretty Boy Floyd, and Alvin Karpis.

"Did you ever heard of the Young Brothers, Jennings and Harry, well known petty criminals in the Springfield area in the early nineteen thirties?" DeMouse asked.

Lefty nodded. "I read somewhere that Harry Young and 'Pretty Boy' Floyd knew each other from serving time in prison at the same time. Floyd was supposed to have visited their farm around the time of the Farm House Massacre."

"The what?" Thomas asked. "Lefty, I knew you and your dad were fascinated with haunts but not with the gangster world. I've lived in Springfield most of my life and I've never heard about the Young Brothers."

"That's a whole other story, Thomas," Lefty said. "Browse the net or I'll fill you in on it sometime after the Fourth."

"I'm beginning to think the Ozarks was a

wild and woolly place."

"This town of Ozark is where a lot of the Young Brothers action started and ended." Lefty glanced at DeMouse, who was unusually quiet. "Did you know Harry's and Jennings' mom and dad are buried in a cemetery right here in Ozark?"

DeMouse nodded, deftly changing the subject. "Sure did, but that was a long time ago. And, that's not why I'm here to receive an award."

"Sir, your grandson, David, told me you were credited with nineteen aces during World War Two!" Thomas said.

DeMouse gave a curt nod as though dismissing that subject, too. "David told me about you, Thomas. Said you had quite a party last night. Sorry I missed it. Sounded like a bang-up time." He wheezed a dry cackle.

"Yeah, the bang-up was my fireworks shell, WONDERMAN. But it was against the law to light it off in the city."

"David said you had a hard time explaining that to the police."

"My step-dad is a private investigator. He stood up for me when they discovered it was my firework shell that had been shot off."

"Didn't you say they are still going to bring the State Fire Marshall's office in to check out the incident?" Lefty asked.

"I'm afraid so. They took the artillery box as evidence." Thomas's tone dropped to a whisper. "I'm not supposed to say anything about this but the display loads are missing, too." Thomas paused. "And, Lefty, remember the bundle of ZEUS firecrackers TNT gave me as a collector's item? The only bundle of five/four hundreds ZEUS ever made?"

Lefty nodded.

"Mom wanted to use them with the WONDERMAN artillery box for her table display and . . ."

"They're gone too?" Lefty finished.

"Yes!"

"If that kook tries to shoot those firecrackers, he's going to hear some loud blasts. They are louder than legal!"

"You don't think this will harm our chances of running the fireworks tent, do you?"

"Probably not if they can prove you didn't have anything to do with shooting fireworks off in the city."

"Weren't you with David and the rest trying to protect your dog when the fireworks started going off?" Pappy asked.

Thomas nodded.

"Well, there's no way you could have been in two places at one time. Tell them about the dog, David said that was quite a show." Pappy said.

"You should have seen David command those dogs," Thomas said.

"The kid takes to animals. When he lived on post with his dad they let him set in on dog command classes. It took his mind off his mom being sick. Last year wasn't the best of years for our family." The old man's voice trailed off.

"He didn't tell me about his mom but he

mentioned he had mono," Thomas said.
"Mononucleosis struck the boy after his
mom passed on. His spleen enlarged and his
dad thought he might lose David, too. Lester
was hoping to be discharged from the Marines
before his wife died but that didn't happen."
His eyes assumed a far away look.

"No wonder his dad worries about him,"
Thomas said.

DeMouse continued, "When Lester got it
into his head to move back to the Ozarks,
David was thrilled. He was even happier when
he found out his dad would be managing an
animal shelter. They have a good father-and-
son relationship. I'm just lucky they include
me inside their family circle."

"Include you?" Thomas asked in wonder.
"David is so proud of you! His dad is too. Why,
you're . . . a real hero!" He nudged Lefty and
grinned. "Not like us boy heroes, who just
lucked into a situation that could be handled
with baseballs."

"You boys are okay!" Pappy's voice grew
serious. "David tells me you're going to be selling fireworks on a farm in Branson."

"That's right! Me and my grandpa are running a tent for Lefty's grandma, TNT."

"Well—" DeMouse's speech was cut short as
their escorts came to accompany them to the
stage.

Alabama wowed the audience with their
special brand of music, spiced up with
Americana. They finished to thunderous
applause.

Now, Thomas, Lefty, and World War II Ace, Pappy DeMouse, stood before a packed stadium of people. Outside the stadium cars honked their horns. Families waved American flags from their car windows.

TNT's voice echoed over the crowd from a mike near the fireworks shooting field, "Before we start the fireworks display, I'd like to say a few words about those two young men and Pappy DeMouse standing on stage . . . "

Lefty nudged Thomas and whispered, "Here comes the speech she's been trying out on me for weeks."

"That your grandma?" Pappy spoke through the side of his mouth without moving a muscle.

"Yes sir!" Lefty said.

"Sounds like a fine woman. I'd be proud to meet her."

"She said the same thing about you! Maybe I can introduce you." Lefty winked at Thomas.

Thomas nodded, thinking Grandpa might want to be there when they are introduced.

Just then the sky lit up with WONDERMAN as he portrayed the hero fighting bad guys and keeping the skies filled with freedom.

The media had been out in force all evening. Radio stations recorded interviews. Television crews taped the presentation of awards. Newspaper reporters scribbled furiously as flash bulbs went off intermittently all evening. Everyone watched as the sky filled with spirals of fiery light celebrating the Fourth of July.

Afterwards, Grandpa, TNT, Carol, Martin, and Wendy were escorted to the stage to be with Lefty and Thomas. Lester and David stood proudly with Pappy DeMouse.

Lefty introduced his grandma to Pappy DeMouse, who in turn, introduced his son and grandson to her.

Thomas did the honors for his family and there was handshaking all around.

Questions and answers about Pappy's years in the Air Force brought cheers from the crowd.

"How many aces do you have to your credit, Pappy?" someone called.

Pappy shrugged and turned to answer another question.

Thomas shouted, "His grandson, David," Thomas patted David on the shoulder, "told me Pappy had nineteen!"

A roar of approval echoed around the stadium.

"Where in the Ozarks do you call home, Pappy?" A woman's voice shrilled.

"Used to be a hilly, curvy road called Branson," Pappy answered.

Thomas saw a group of his friends working their way to the front of the crowd. When they finally stood near the edge of the stage, he reached down and handed each of them a miniature terrier resembling GFF, complete with a flag on its collar.

"The National Animal Shelter Foundation had these stuffed animals made to resemble their Poster Dog. They are selling them for keepsakes. The proceeds go to animal shelters." Thomas grinned. "They call the stuffed animal Freddie Freedom. GFF has a namesake.

We've got a basket full to toss to the crowd."

Thomas pitched some of the dogs high above the crowd.

The crowd begged for more yelling, "Thomas, Thomas!"

Lefty grabbed up a few. He pointed to people in the crowd. Then he assumed his pitching stance, wound up, and hurled the animal to them. Soon, the crowd was cheering, "Slider, Slider!" remembering the fireworks named for Lefty.

"Hey, Thomas, why did they call the fireworks named for you WONDERMAN?" A voice called.

"That used to be the password for my computer. And I dig super heros."

"Where can I buy a WONDERMAN and SLIDER fireworks shell?" A man called.

"At most fireworks tents." Thomas glanced at TNT and Grandpa.

They both nodded with a smile.

"Hey, come on down to Branson. Me and my grandpa are running a tent for TNT there! We'll be open starting next Wednesday. Only four more days!"

Friendly voices continued to toss questions to the guests of honor on the stage.

Alabama and The Ozark Mountain Daredevils packed up their gear and their buses preparing to leave.

As the crowd dispersed, a shrill voice called from the back of the group, "Thomas Scott!"

Thomas peered into the glare of the ballpark lights trying to see the person.

"Have you got to shoot off your WONDER-MAN shell?"

"Yep!"

"I thought so! I saw it last night. It really got a lot of attention in Springfield."

Chitchat ceased on the stage as everyone turned to see who was shouting the accusation.

"I didn't . . ."

"Yeah, I heard that's what you tried to tell the cops." A sneer coated the voice.

"Rat-a-tat! Boom! Rat-a-tat! Boom!" Flashes of light flickered across the ground as the unmistakable sound of super loud firecrackers blasted and flashed, scattering the remaining crowd.

Screams, yells, and shouts filled the stadium as people pushed and shoved each other trying to get away from the bursts of powder as the firecrackers shot in every direction.

Martin vaulted off the stage and moved toward the area.

From his vantage point Thomas saw a figure pushing and shoving its way toward the edge of the crowd. Suddenly the figure broke free and started running toward the area where automobiles were trying to edge their way into the long line of departing vehicles.

"How long will the firecrackers last?" Pappy asked.

"Those firecrackers can only be ZEUS brand," Lefty said in a hushed voice. He peered over his shoulder at his grandma. "They have too much powder to pass customs if someone was going to sell them. TNT is going to be hot if it's Thomas's stolen four hundreds. We can only hope that loser lit only one package of them or this riot could go on forever."

Thomas felt a sick lurch of his stomach at Lefty's words. "TNT is going to be hot!"

Anger rose in his throat at events beyond his control. Releasing pent up fury, he yelled, "He's crazy shooting them right in the middle of the crowd! Why would he put people in danger just to get back at me?"

"There must be two of them if it's the same scum from last night," Grandpa said. "Let's get off this stage. We're sitting ducks. Let Martin take care if it."

Grandpa muttered something in a low voice to one of the men assigned to escort their group. Putting an arm across Thomas and Lefty's shoulders, he eased them closer to Carol, Wendy, and TNT.

The security man quickly herded all of them toward the steps at the back of the stage. "Come on folks. I'm moving you to the Ducks dressing room." He spoke into his cupped hand. In minutes other security men surrounded the group moving them along.

Sirens came nearer. Flashing lights illuminated the side road leading to the four lane highway beyond.

"Oh, wow!" Thomas gasped, as the traveling bus carrying Alabama barely avoided a pile up as it swerved to miss a run-away pickup.

A green pickup jumped a ditch, tore through a fence, and moved toward the back of a residential area.

"Lefty! David!" Thomas said just before they were ushered into the confines of the Ducks dressing room. "See, it's Jervis's green pickup!"

The ball park lights reflected off a motorcycle trail. It wound along a tall, flag-draped, fence separating a sub-division from the chaos of the ball park area. Bouncing over ruts and ditches, the pickup sped over the uneven ground like a rat searching for the end of a maze.

Suddenly, it found an opening. With a squeal of its brakes it made a quick turn. The tail gate broke free. It flapped up and down as the tail lights disappeared from view.

Pappy DeMouse moved closer to Thomas, "Kid, you've made some ruthless enemies!"

Martin ran toward them.

Carol uttered a cry and ran into his arms.

As the group entered the safety of the building, Martin handed Thomas a torn piece of red firecracker paper. Part of a label revealed the mighty ZEUS with lightning rod extended.

Tears blurred Thomas eyes as he looked up directly into TNT's piercing stare. She looked hot!

Chapter 9
Opening Day

"Can you believe Jervis claimed his pickup was stolen Saturday afternoon?" Thomas asked Grandpa for the umteenth time.

"How convenient!" Grandpa gave Thomas a long-suffering look. They had talked this subject to death while they helped the crew set up the tent in Branson.

But Thomas persisted. "At least when Jervis was driving that old green pickup we knew what to look for. Now, who knows what he might show up in?"

"Thomas!" Grandpa said sternly. "Jervis won't be showing up down here."

"But. . ."

"No buts about it! Martin is staking out Jervis. Lester and David are going to back him up. And, they are making sure Jervis knows it. He's going to get a taste of his own medicine. Everywhere Jervis goes, they go! They are going to keep that man so busy he won't even have time to think about you not being around." Grandpa sipped a cola and continued, "Somewhere along the way Jervis will make a mistake. The sheriff's men will nab him."

"Why can't the sheriff just arrest him?"

"It's like Martin said, they can't prove he or his son did anything wrong. In fact, they can't even find his son. Jervis claims he ran off." Grandpa stopped to stroke his chin. "So far those two were just in the wrong place at the right time."

"Some coincidence! A man and a boy destroy our Fourth of July party, shoot off our fireworks, and then steal the rest. At the same time Jervis's pickup is parked near our house. He claims he and his son are walking their dogs." Thomas sighed. "Then firecrackers like the ones stolen from our back yard are shot off in a crowd of people at the Duck Stadium where we just happen to be on stage receiving an award." Thomas raised his hands palms up in a 'can you believe it' gesture.

"Jervis's pickup roars out of the parking lot almost causing a wreck." Thomas holds up one finger as though making an amazing discovery. "But, of course, that pickup was stolen Saturday afternoon, and he conveniently forgot to report it to the police."

Thomas rolled his eyes expressing disbelief. "Too bad I couldn't see who it was that hollered at me Saturday night before they shot off the fireworks."

"Too bad, too bad!" Grandpa shook his head. "Too bad Carol didn't get a better look at them that night in the back yard."

"This is really hard on Mom. She blames herself for asking to use my fireworks for a display on the table. She told TNT she didn't know the ZEUS firecrackers were a collector's item or she'd never have asked to use them at the party."

Grandpa gave a dry chuckle, "You are one lucky boy. TNT was ready to lower the boom on you for being careless. She's hoping Martin can get the WONDERMAN fireworks and the rest of the ZEUS fireworks back without further incident."

"Me too!" A pained expression flickered across Thomas's face.

Grandpa hammered the stake one last time. "When she found out you didn't just leave those fireworks laying around but your mom had asked to use them for display, she backed off."

Thomas nodded. "I can't believe we're finally here and the tent is up! Doesn't it look great?" Thomas stood by the yellow and red striped tent. The vinyl lifted slightly as a stray breeze battled the blistering heat and teased the side curtains. Cars passing on the highway honked a friendly greeting.

Thomas moved toward the camper. "I'm going to see if GFF is okay."

"He's probably doing better than we are. It's air conditioned in there. Hurry back. We need to help unload the rest of this stuff and get it set up."

TNT's crew showed Thomas how to staple red, white, and blue bunting around the bottom of the tables. Soon the lights were strung around the top of the tent. Tables were ready for the fireworks. The crew unloaded the last of the cases.

"Any questions before we take off?" the crew manager asked.

"I think we've got it under control. All we need now are customers," Grandpa said.

"Thanks for everything."

"Remember to keep your ropes tightened. Roll up your flaps during the day, and if it starts to rain—" He stopped as everyone began to laugh. Shielding his eyes with his hand, he peered up at the blistering sun and sighed. "Well, that may be one thing you don't have to worry about. But, during fireworks season you need to be ready for anything." He raised a hand gesturing farewell as he climbed into the cab and pulled away.

The next hours were spent pricing, putting up no smoking signs, and marking the entrance for customers.

"Give it a rest!" Grandpa said, as Thomas checked once more to be sure he had price signs on the inside and outside of the tables. Finally, they were ready to do business! Everything was in place but their watchdog.

Grandpa moved some lawn chairs outside under the small awning of the camper. Thomas slipped GFF's run-a-round lease over the top of a stake.

They had just sat down to admire their tent when a car pulled in. Kids spilled out and scrambled over each other running for the tent. A young woman hollered at them to wait as she followed close on their heels.

"Looks like our first customers have arrived!" Grandpa said as he and Thomas hurried toward the tent with GFF barking up a storm.

The sun was sinking in the west when they finally got to sit down.

"I never thought I'd get tired of telling people what the WONDERMAN shell does." Thomas sighed heavily as he sank down beside GFF and ruffled his fur.

"It's too early in the season to get tired, boy." Grandpa wiped his forehead with his handkerchief. "You hungry? I guess we should grab a bite before another car comes."

"Hungry, are you?" A gruff voice asked.

GFF yipped a startled bark just as the tall gaunt figure of Harley Jones emerged from behind the camper with a big, brown paper sack in his hand.

Grandpa jerked upright. "Harley! Good to see you!"

"Hi, Mister Jones. What do you think of our dog?" Thomas pulled GFF toward him by his lease rope.

"Spunky little thing." Harley chuckled. "Where did you get a bit of fur like that?"

"It's a long story. Sit down and we'll tell you about it," Grandpa offered.

Harley dropped into one of the chairs and deposited his bag on a small patio table. "I got time for a story if you got time for some bologna and cheese sandwiches." He reached into the bag and pulled out some sandwiches and a bag of chips.

While they ate, Harley listened to the story of how GFF came to live with Thomas and the troubles that followed.

"And, you think the man causing all the problems was this Jervis who worked at the pound?" Harley asked as he reached for another chip.

Thomas nodded as he chewed.

"Seems so. Thomas's step-father, Martin, is a private detective. He, Lester, and David, Pappy DeMouse's son and grandson, are going to keep him under surveillance while we're down here."

"I hope they get enough evidence to arrest him. Martin was going to come down and help us. Lester and David might come with him." Thomas washed down the last of his meal with a cola. "They might even bring Pappy. Wouldn't you like to meet the man who shot down nineteen planes during World War Two, Mister Jones?"

"Sure would! I used to read about things like that in the newspaper a long time ago." He paused. "Things are getting lively around here. I watched from my porch while you all set your tent and put your fireworks out to sell."

"I hope we aren't bothering you," Grandpa said.

"Nope. I'm enjoying the company. I didn't know how lonesome I was till you two visited the other day." Harley gulped his cola. "Sorry I got carried away telling about days that are best forgot."

"It's okay," Grandpa and Thomas said in unison.

"Guess I better get on back home." Harley's bones cracked as he stood. "Thomas, you still want to play ball at my barn?"

Thomas jumped up so fast GFF began to yip. "Sure, Mister Jones."

"Tell you what, if your grandpa can spare you for a bit why don't you and your dog walk back with me. We'll stop at the barn. I've got something to show you." Harley's wrinkled face smoothed with a grin.

Thomas's eyes held a question when he looked at his grandpa.

"Sure, you and GFF go ahead. I can handle any customers who might wander in." Grandpa grinned.

Thomas matched his steps with the old man as they walked through the meadow toward the old barn. Almost lost in the tall, dry grass, GFF yipped at their heels.

"Well, what do you think?" Harley said as he flipped a switch flooding the barn with light.

Thomas turned in circles trying to take in the changes. "Gosh! I thought it was cool before. How did you get all this done so fast?" His gaze traveled over the official score board mounted high above. Chairs were lined up for players on both sides of the score keeper's table. There was even a basketball carrier full of new basketballs.

"You said you needed to practice for a big tournament. I thought you might invite your team down here. I didn't want you to be ashamed of the court." Harley watched Thomas closely. "Now son, don't feel like you got to do anything if you don't want to."

"No, no!" Thomas's voice caught in his throat thinking how much time and money the old man had spent getting this ready for him.

Harley wheezed an embarrassed cough.

"Sorry, it's probably not good enough."

"Mister Jones, this is one of the best courts I've ever seen. I'd be proud to have anyone play here. You bet I'll ask my team to practice." He hesitated. "And, we'd like to have you watch."

A big smile lit up Harley's face. "Truth is, Thomas, I was hoping you'd ask me. I don't like to keep mentioning it, but it's going to be nice to have young people on this old farm again."

"Yip, yip, yip-yip-yip!" GFF ran from the side of the building where the barn was still a barn. He came to a halt in front of Thomas jumping to be picked up.

Thomas reached to pull him up. "What's the matter, boy? Did something scare you?" Thomas peered into the dark recesses of the barn. Just for an instance he thought he saw a pair of golden eyes staring back at him.

A low growl began in GFF's throat. He scrambled closer in Thomas's arms.

"Probably that old tom cat that was hanging around while the men were working on the court," Harley muttered. "Guess we better call it a night. Don't want your grandpa getting worried about you."

Dusk was claiming the horizon and the evening seemed degrees cooler when they emerged from the barn.

"Look!" Thomas gasped, as he pointed toward the fireworks tent.

"Quite a sight!" Harley exclaimed.

In the distance the fireworks tent was outlined against the evening sky with lights around the outside. The inside lights illuminated the red and yellow striped walls giving the area a magic glow.

Thomas could hardly wait to get back to the tent and see if it looked as good on the inside as it did outside. "Mister Jones, do you want me and GFF to walk you back to your house?"

"Thanks, but I've walked these fields many a time. You and your dog get back and help your grandpa." He waved and started toward his house. Then he turned back. "And, don't forget! While you're here that barn's yours to use anytime."

"Thanks!" Thomas called, as he ran with GFF through the grassy field toward the fireworks tent.

"GRRROWL!" The eerie sound claimed the countryside. It started near the barn and carried into the trees behind, over the meadow closer and closer to Thomas as he ran faster and faster with GFF held tightly in his arms.

"Hold on!" Strong arms grabbed him just as he reached the clearing back of the camper.

Thomas screamed, clutching GFF tighter.

"Are you all right? What happened?" Grandpa pulled Thomas and GFF into a tight hug.

"Grandpa!" Relief spread a warm glow throughout Thomas's body.

Inside the tent with the lights burning brightly, Thomas felt foolish. What had spooked him? Had the stories the old man told the first time they met come back to haunt him?

"So, you and GFF let a cat scare you?"

Grandpa teased as he eased the side curtains down getting ready to close for the night. "Why don't you go tie GFF up and let's get some sleep. Tomorrow will be here before we know it."

Thomas looked toward the black outline of the barn in the distance. Just then the windows of the old man's house came alive with light.

Thomas led GFF back to the tethered pole and started to snap his collar to the fastener, but GFF growled low in his throat and edged closer to Thomas.

"I know, GFF. It didn't sound like any cat I've ever heard."

Thomas picked up the little dog and held him close.

Suddenly, the tent lights went out. Immediately, a glow flickered near the tent and began to move toward them.

As Thomas clutched the dog closer, he became aware of the country night sounds. A low buzzing of crickets combined with distant hoots. Fireflies blinked an SOS of day's end. As his eyes adjusted to the darkness, Thomas saw an outline of his grandpa materializing from the gloom.

"Grandpa, do you think it would be okay if GFF slept with me tonight?"

Light flooded Thomas's face as Grandpa turned the flashlight upward. "You sure you're okay?"

"Yep." Thomas clutched the little terrier close.

"What did Harley show you?"

"I'll tell you later. Please, can I bring GFF inside?"

"Sure, bring the dog on in," Grandpa chortled. "GFF, General Freddie Freedom. Some watchdog!"

Chapter 10
Security

Inside the camper, Thomas finished telling Grandpa about his visit with Harley and all the work the old man had done on his barn. "Do you think the Panthers will come down and practice at Harley's barn?"

"I'd say he'd be pretty disappointed if they don't. I'd like to walk up there and look around."

"Tonight?" The alarm in Thomas's voice made GFF start to growl.

"That cat really scared you, didn't it? How about we mosey up that way before we open in the morning?" Grandpa suggested.

Thomas nodded. He started to set up his laptop on the table by the window nearest the fireworks tent. "We're so close to the tent it's like the camper is actually a part of it."

"That's the idea. TNT told me a lot of the managers sleep in their tents for security reasons. But our tent is hot as an oven with the side curtains down. I'd hate to try to sleep in there." Grandpa stretched out on his bunk holding something that looked like the remote for the television.

"Will we be able to hear if someone tries to break in the tent during the night?"

"This apparatus," Grandpa held the instrument up, "is the remote control for a security system I set up while you were at the barn with

Harley." He pointed the remote towards the tent. "When I activate the current that surrounds the tent, it triggers invisible lasers. If anyone tries to cross the area, sirens and bells go off and lights will start flashing. The security people will dispatch a patrol to help us out."

"Wow! I should have been here to help you!"

"Naw, it didn't take long. Once I got it rigged up I called the security people and they came by. It's okay!"

"Turn it on. I'll watch and see if I can tell any difference." Thomas edged nearer the window peering at the tent in the semi-darkness beyond.

"Here goes!" Grandpa pressed a button on the remote where a red light blinked and remained on.

"Go ahead, I'm waiting," Thomas called.

"It's on."

"I didn't see anything happen. Wait a minute!" Thomas stuck his nose against the window pane. "There's a rabbit! It's moving toward the tent. It'll set off the alarm, Grandpa!"

GFF, alarmed by the anxiety in Thomas's voice, started barking and trying to climb Thomas's leg.

"Calm down, both of you! It would take something bigger than a rabbit." He reached over and picked up GFF. "Or you, little dog, to set off this alarm."

Thomas turned from the window, a look of suspicion on his face. "Grandpa, I thought you didn't think Jervis would come down to

Branson."

Grandpa's face flushed. "Now, Thomas . . . "

"Admit it! That security system is meant to catch Jervis, isn't it?"

"The truth is, Martin and Carol wouldn't let me bring you if we didn't take every precaution. They knew you had your heart set on helping with this tent. Martin sent this with me and made arrangements with the security people."

"He's pretty cool, isn't he?"

"Sure is. You're lucky to have him as part of your family." He handed GFF to Thomas and laid back on his bunk. "Think I'll catch the news."

"I'm going to check my email." Thomas patted GFF, who had stretched out on his lap.

You have mail! He scanned the long list of incoming messages.

Ahunk, Wendy, Jodie, Martin, a few of his Panther teammates, Lefty, and one from David!

He accessed Martin's message. *Thomas: Lester, David, and I keep close tabs on Jervis through our binoculars. We've never seen his son. I guess he's still gone.*

"Wow!"

Lester checked out the medicine bottle Jervis dropped at the animal shelter. That drug is highly neuro-toxic and brain disabling. Prolonged intake of it can cause disruption of normal brain function and influence a patient's ability to think and act.

"Grandpa, listen to this." Thomas read the beginning of Martin's email and continued to the end.

We'd love to get inside the house but we don't have enough evidence for a search warrant. Lester says if we can get in the backyard we may be able to prove some of dogs are stolen from the animal shelter.

Please be careful. I'm doing a complete computer search of Jervis. I'll keep you posted. I sent some things with Grandpa to help out with your security system.

Grandpa chuckled. "Good thing I let you in on the security system. You'd have found out anyway."

"You didn't . . ." Thomas stopped, knowing Grandpa was teasing. "Hey listen, we're going to have reinforcements for the weekend!"

Lester, David, and Pappy are going to be decoys for me this weekend so I can slip down to Branson and bring Wendy. She's pestering us to get down there and help. Your mom sends her love. Martin.

"Good! TNT says the weekends are generally busy." Grandpa turned the news up a notch as the weather report began.

Thomas heard, ". . . heat wave continues . . ." Then, he accessed AHunk's email.

AHunk wrote, *June 20, How was opening day? This time next week we'll be there to help you sell fireworks!*

Thomas said, "We?"

You probably noticed I said 'we'! I'm bringing a friend. I think you'll be impressed with Kaylene. I hope you don't mind that I told her . . .

"Her?" Thomas grinned.

. . . the old man's story about his boys and

their dog disappearing years ago on the very farm where we'll be selling fireworks. Kaylene is sensitive to things like this and is anxious to visit the place.

"Sensitive?" Thomas whispered.

I've told her so much about you and your family. I made reservations for us at the Chateau on the Lake. We're going to take in some sights at Branson after the Fourth. Then we'll head on down to your AAU Tournament at Florida.

"She's going to Florida, too?" Thomas exclaimed.

"What are you mumbling about?" Grandpa asked.

"Sydney's got a girl friend!" Thomas repeated Sydney's news.

"Sensitive, eh? Hope he's not mixed up with one of those crystal ball women! If he is, Harley will run them off, and maybe us, too!"

"I'll email and tell him what you said."

"Better not. Sydney's a smart guy. He'll handle it." Grandpa switched off the television just as the phone rang.

"I'll get it!" Thomas reached for the phone.

"Don't pick up that phone!" Grandpa was up in a flash grabbing the phone from Thomas. "Look at the caller ID before you answer, remember?"

"So, who is it?"

Grandpa sank back down on the bed and handed the phone to Thomas. "It your house number. It's probably your mom."

"Hi Mom? What's happening?" Thomas listened more than he talked. He rolled his eyes at Grandpa, grinned, shrugged, and kept repeating, "Yeah, sure." Finally, he said, "Me, too," and hung up.

"Everything okay?"

"Yep, She's just worried and wanted to be sure I wasn't disappointed that she wasn't coming with Martin and Wendy this weekend."

"It's too hot for her down here."

"Sure."

"We better get some sleep."

"I've just got a few more emails to check. Then GFF and I'll turn in, okay?"

"Okay." Grandpa turned his head away from the light and was soon snoring.

Thomas read the rest of his emails quickly. He answered them just as quickly.

To the Panthers, he wrote: *Get the coach to bring the team down here to practice Sunday. You won't believe the court the old man has fixed up for us!*

To Wendy: *Glad you're coming down this weekend. You're going to like this place.*

To Sydney: *I can't believe you've finally got a girl friend!*

Grandpa and I can't wait to meet Kaylene. Please be careful about any weird stuff on old man Jones's farm. It'll be good to see you. I've got a lot to tell you.

Thomas's fingers flew over the keyboard. He told Sydney everything that happened starting with the ruined fireworks party, the incident at the Ducks Stadium, and about the barn Harley had fixed for him. He even told him the scary part about the crazy sound that seemed to be chasing him and GFF. He ended with the security system and Martin's email about Jervis's medicine.

"Sydney, get here soon!" he whispered.

David's email was filled with information about watching Jervis and wishing they were with Thomas.

Thomas answered Jodie's questions and told her to come down with the Panthers.

Briefly, he answered Martin's questions and told him he'd be glad to see him and Wendy when they came down this weekend.

Thomas got up to stretch. He walked to the fridge to get a cold drink. Bending down, he looked out the window that faced the old barn. Moonlight played over the tall roof of the barn, caressed the weathered boards, slid down to the grassy field, and raced away to the trees beyond.

"What the . . . " Thomas stared at the shape of a large animal loping toward the tree line. Suddenly, it was swallowed up by the forest. Thomas tried to remember what Harley had told them was at the back of his property.

"A cemetery!" he whispered. "A cemetery that ended in a bluff that fell to the river below." A chill passed over his shoulder causing him to shiver. Shaking it off, he returned to his laptop.

He read Lefty's email. *Everything is going great at our tent. I hope you remembered to activate the security software I gave you.*

Thomas slapped a hand against his forehead as he withdrew Lefty's CD and inserted it into his computer.

"WOW!" Thomas repeated the word so often and with such feeling GFF soon tired of rousting. He turned his back on Thomas.

Thomas downloaded, studied, reset, adjusted, and followed instructions. Finally he had scaled the program to fit their tent size. In bold letters he wrote, THOMAS SCOTT AND TOM SCOTT'S FIREWORKS TENT. Holding his breath, he clicked the SEND button.

Like a huge movie screen, the words transferred themselves onto the tent top. Thomas moved the letters to different parts of the tent. To the top center pole, over the side curtains, and to the sky above the tent.

Quickly, he entered a string of commands and pushed SEND.

Outside a loud voice announced, "Thomas Scott and Tom Scott's Fireworks tent!" Thomas jammed his finger down on ESC and the voice quit.

"GFF? Did you hear it? We've got audio!" Thomas checked to see if the noise had wakened his grandpa. Satisfied it hadn't, he turned once more to his laptop.

Scanning a fireworks label, he enlarged the picture of a Black Cat's head to mammoth size. He pressed SEND and gasped as the huge cat's yellow eyes stared back at him from the top of the tent. Like a demon, it perched there ready to pounce, teeth bared, and nostrils flared!

"Excellent!" he said, preparing to turn on a recording of a wild cat's yowl.

"Thomas! Is something wrong?" Grandpa had turned toward him and was rubbing sleep from his eyes.

Thomas jumped. He removed his finger from the SEND button. "Go back to sleep, Grandpa. I'll show you tomorrow. I've been working with the software TNT and Lefty gave us. It's so cool!"

"Yowlll!" The noise from outside caused Thomas to jump. Had he accidentally pushed the sound button?

He looked at the image of the Black Cat, expecting to see it had come to life and shrieked at him. But, it sat exactly as he'd left it.

"Yowll!" The cry was closer. Thomas's heart jumped to his throat.

Quickly, he snapped off the program. The cat disappeared from the tent. He looked to see if Grandpa had heard the shrieking sound, but sleep had claimed him once more. Even GFF slept.

Thomas waited. In the distance, toward the back of the property, beyond the trees, the cry sounded again. Then it faded and was gone.

Thomas bent to his computer and began to write. *Lefty, I wish you were here. You are not going to believe . . .*

He stopped writing, closed his computer, turned off the light, and stretched out on his bed.

If anyone would believe him, it would be Lefty. He remembered Lefty saying, "You can activate my new security software. It'll project an image in infra-red light on a selected spot on your tent. Wallah! Call nine-one-one! Or turn CC loose on them."

Something jumped on his bed!

Thomas jerked away before realizing it was the little terrier. "GFF! If only you were bigger and meaner like CC."

Chapter 11

Tattoo

"What a weekend!" Thomas's jersey and shorts were sweaty. He'd just finished a two-hour basketball practice with the Panthers. "Too bad Martin and Wendy had to leave. But, I'm glad David came with them."

"They were good help while you and David were at Harley's barn this afternoon." Grandpa stood in front of the big fan trying to get cool.

"When everyone saw the outside of the barn they were dumbfounded." Thomas mimicked them, "You expect us to practice in this?"

"I bet they changed their tune when they went inside." Grandpa whistled a 'Wow' between his teeth. "They couldn't have been any more surprised than I when I saw the changes this morning."

Thomas pulled a case of fireworks from beneath the counter and plopped on top of it. "The kids thought Harley and the barn were awesome."

"Having a bunch of kids playing ball in that barn again must have been traumatic for Harley," Grandpa said, "Did he say anything about his missing boys and the dog?"

"He said he'd remember David and Skeeter Jones cause they had the same last name as him. He told David he once had a son called Dave."

"What did David say?" Grandpa asked.

"He asked if he had any more sons. Harley

said he had two, Mick and Dave, but they were both gone."

"I guess he's finally admitted they're not coming back. Now maybe he can find closure." Grandpa fanned his T-shirt to let some cool air beneath it.

"Remember how he dribbled the basketball and shot the first day we were here?" Thomas asked.

Grandpa nodded. "I was surprised he was in such good condition. I bet he spends a lot of time in that barn."

"Harley challenged David to a game of HORSE while we were doing some drills." Thomas ran a hand through his damp hair. "David is good! But Harley almost beat him."

Grandpa laughed. "You think your team's about ready for Nationals?"

Thomas moved to another part of the counter. "We better be. The tournament is the second week in July."

"You all leaving two weeks from today?"

"Yep, right after the Fourth! Hey, what did you think of Lefty's software I installed?"

"The first time that Black Cat shrieked I about went through the top of the tent." Grandpa chuckled. "It's funny how you can record and have it talk to the customers."

"I programed it to work with the security system you set up. Remember how Lefty said it could project the image of a bugler on the side of the tent and call nine-one-one?"

"We're already set to call security," Grandpa said.

"I know, but now a voice is going to shout a pre-recorded message, 'You're surrounded. Give it up! Last warning before we shoot!'" Thomas laughed.

"Dehumanized mechanics! What will they think of next?" Grandpa grunted. "Restock the punks at the checkout stand and get some more smoke bombs. Here comes another bunch of cars."

The Sunday evening crowd milled the aisles checking prices.

"What does this do?" Two kids prowled up and down the counters.

"How much is this?" the woman asked ignoring the price card.

Thomas reached beneath the counter and pushed a button. The mammoth Black Cat head he'd programmed to appear near the top of the tent cried, "Meowwwwwwww!"

"Look it, a Black Cat!" the kids yelled.

A loud voice near the Cat announced, "Everything is marked on cards in front of the merchandise."

"Cool!" The kids continued pestering their parents to fill their baskets.

Thomas finished refilling the smoke bombs and straightened the bottle rockets.

The voice announced, "WONDERMAN is a artillery shell named after Thomas Scott. Ask him, he'll be glad to tell you about it."

Thomas looked up quickly to see Grandpa moving away from the button that activated the sound.

"Are you Thomas? Is this Super Hero shell

really named after you? Tell me . . ." Thomas heard Grandpa chuckling as he sacked fireworks and collected money. It was evident who had programmed that message.

Thomas had just turned on the outside tent lights when a Jeep with four tough-looking men drove up.

Grandpa greeted them. "Can we help you?"

"Just looking," the man with tattoos covering his arms snapped, pulling a pack of cigarettes and a lighter from his pocket.

Thomas pointed at the 'No Smoking' signs. "Sir, no one can smoke in or around this tent."

The man scowled but stuck the items back in his pocket. "Sure, kid."

One man lurked near the entrance while Tattoo moved to the back of the tent. The other two split up roaming the aisles, picking up and discarding fireworks as they prowled.

Grandpa frowned a warning to Thomas to watch one end of the counter while he positioned himself to watch the other.

"How much are your M-Eighties?" Tattoo asked.

Thomas reached for the button to tell them everything was marked.

Grandpa stopped him with a shake of his head. "Signs are in front of the merchandise."

From the corner of his eye, Thomas saw one of the guys pull a bottle from his back pocket and take a big swig before he replaced it.

Grandpa moved to stand near Tattoo.

"Tell me about these cones, boy," the man with the bottle demanded.

While Thomas explained the different sized cones, the other two men moved to the end of the counter by the camper. Thomas kept talking and moved back where he could see the other two.

"What you looking at, boy? You gonna finish telling me about these cones, or not?" The man screwed up his mouth, hawked, and spit on the floor.

"You and the boy by yourselves, Gramps?" Tattoo asked.

Thomas saw Grandpa reach beneath the counter. He knew the gun was there.

"We got plenty of help. Why?" Grandpa kept his hand hidden.

"Me and my friends were looking for work. Just thought you might need some help. Right boys?" He laughed.

Their loud laughter rang out over the meadow where shadows claimed the landscape.

"Yip, yip-yip!" GFF's growl followed his barks.

"Sounds like you got a watchdog," Tattoo said, looking toward the camper where GFF was tethered in the dusk.

"Yep, big old black dog," Grandpa lied.

Thomas looked at Grandpa in surprise. Grandpa shook his head slightly in warning.

"Sounds like a little squirt. Maybe we better check him out."

"If you guys need fireworks, buy them and get on your way. I wouldn't mess with that dog if I were you." Grandpa's voice had taken on a hard edge.

Thomas fidgeted, wondering what he could do to help. Suddenly he remembered Lefty's software could project images on the tent. He moseyed toward the buttons talking as he moved, "Let me show you the WONDERMAN artillery shell . . ."

"Stay where you are, boy!" One of the men ordered. "Go check out the dog, Tony."

Tony went outside the tent toward the camper.

"Yowlllll!" The shrill cry sounded near the barn and moved toward the tent as Thomas reached for the buttons. Startled, he jerked his hand back.

Grandpa whirled toward Thomas and the men. He arm was extended holding the handgun.

Tattoo held up his hands and backed off. "Now Gramps, don't get excited. That thing might go off." He motioned for the others to join him near the entrance.

"Yowllll-lll!"

"Grrr!"

"Helpppp!" The man's voice came from near GFF's pole.

"Come on, Tony! Let's get out of here," Tattoo yelled.

"Get off me!" Tony squalled a thin, high, scream.

Tattoo and the other two man scrambled through the entrance and out to their Jeep.

Thomas pushed the button to activate the voice. It boomed, "You're surrounded. Give it up! Last warning before we shoot!"

"Waitttt!" Tony stumbled into the light trying to get to the Jeep. His shirt was torn. His jeans were ripped. His bloody fingers were clamped around his upper arm.

The motor of the Jeep came to life as hands reached to haul Tony inside.

Grandpa stepped to the entrance and yelled, "Don't come back! We've called the cops!"

The Jeep hit the highway screeching its tires and roared into the dark.

Grandpa turned with the gun held in front of him.

"Grandpa!" Thomas gasped.

"Sorry!" Grandpa lowered the gun placing it beneath the counter. Sweat grooved the side of his face. He collapsed on nearest box. "Are you all right?"

"Yes, what about you?" Thomas's jersey and shorts stuck to him like a second skin. He flipped the switch on the tent pole that turned on the camper light near GFF's pole and gasped, "Oh no!"

GFF was huddled against his pole. His white fur was matted with blood. Behind him a humongous shadow loomed against the camper.

"GFF! You're hurt!" Thomas lunged for the entrance.

"Thomas!" Grandpa's voice was razor-sharp. "Don't go out there. It took something mighty big to mess that man up. Let me get the gun."

"Yowlll!" The cry sounded behind the camper.

"Yip, yip!" GFF warned.

Thomas moved back to the buttons that controlled Lefty's software. He switched on the Image Alert. "If anyone or anything is out there we'll know in a second." Instantly, the side of the tent lit up with a blinding flash outlining a gigantic shadow against the yellow and red vinyl.

"What are you doing?" Grandpa held the gun down by his side.

"Just a minute." He maneuvered the light away from the tent and onto the camper.

"Yowlll!" The cry moved swiftly away. As it retreated, Thomas gauged its withdrawal from across the meadow, to the barn and over the clearing to the trees. Then it was gone.

"Come on, Grandpa! It's safe. We've got to get to GFF!" Thomas ran through the entrance and out to the camper.

Sirens in the distance came closer as Grandpa joined Thomas to examine the little terrier.

Security men checked out the grounds even after being told the men had left in a Jeep.

"Can't be too careful," the man said, drawing out his notebook and pencil. "I'm going to make a few notes. You tell me exactly what happened."

While Grandpa repeated the story once more, Thomas showed the other man GFF's pole and explained the little dog wasn't hurt but he was covered with blood.

"From what you've said, I'd say that man you called Tony saved your terrier from being some coyote's dinner."

Thomas cringed and pulled GFF to him. "You mean you think a coyote was going to attack GFF and got Tony instead?"

The man nodded and walked inside.

The security men compared notes as Thomas and Grandpa prepared to close the tent for the night. GFF followed close on Thomas's heels as he helped Grandpa unroll the side curtains.

"Mister Scott?" one of the men called.

Grandpa turned.

"We know you have your security system ready to turn on after you close, but what exactly did you have on tonight?"

Grandpa looked at Thomas and nodded.

Thomas showed the men Lefty's software and explained how it worked.

The man scoffed, "You're telling me this gadget can pick out an image and reflect it on the tent?"

Thomas nodded.

"Does it save the image?"

"I'm not sure. I've never tried that." He fiddled with the instrument. He pushed a button and the light flashed on the side curtains.

Everyone turned to stare. An oversized shadow covered most of the area with a blurry image suspended in the background.

"What's this?" the security man asked.

"The vision reflected when I turned on the alert alarm. This was the area near GFF's tether pole by the camper.

"Is there any way you can get us a copy of

that?"

Thomas slipped a CD into the instrument and punched in some instructions. The machine whirred. He ejected the CD and handed it to the man. "What are you going to do with it?"

"I'd like to take it to the lab and have our experts go over it."

"Let us know what you find out," Grandpa said.

"You bet." Swiping his sweaty face with his sleeve, he said, "I think we've done everything we can here. You and the boy going to be okay? Or should we leave someone to watch for tonight?"

Grandpa looked at Thomas. "You scared?"

Thomas clutched GFF in his arms. "GFF is going to stay inside, right?"

"From now on GFF stays close to us."

"Then, I think we'll be okay. You guys got here pretty quick last time."

"Okay, we'll make our report and get this CD checked out." They waved. "Call us if those guys come back."

"It's not those guys I'm afraid will come back," Grandpa said, locking the camper door after they were inside.

Thomas hosed the blood off GFF in the camper sink. "Grandpa. How big do you think that thing is?"

Grandpa shook his head. "Too big!"

"Yip, yip-yip!" GFF complained as the water dripping from his fur turned red and ran down the drain.

Later, Thomas finished typing Ahunk an email. *Please run this through your sensitizer and let me know what you find out.* He detailed the events of the night and attached a copy of the hulking shadow and the outline behind it. He went to bed certain he'd hear from his friend by morning.

Next morning, a cheerful voice from Thomas's laptop announced, "You have mail."

He checked a list of incoming messages.

There it was. Ahunk! *Thomas, I'm sending this to a apparitional lab. Kaylene and I have both examined it and we agree the huge shadow is the shape of a oversized dog. The outline behind it is too blurry to make out but Kaylene feels it's a young boy.*

Thomas felt a cold chill creep down his back. For some strange reason the words, "Oink, oink, croak, hee-haw," flickered across his mind.

From what you've told us about the farm where your tent is located, Kaylene feels there may be restless spirits on the prowl. Kaylene and I will be there in a few days, maybe sooner.

GFF yipped as Grandpa entered the camper closing the outside door on a blast of hot air. "Let's get a move on. It's time to open the tent." He looked closely at Thomas. "You look like you've seen a ghost!"

"Look at this!" Thomas turned the monitor where Grandpa could read what Ahunk had written.

Grandpa scowled. "That's all we need, spirits on the prowl. It's not enough we've got a stalker, who Martin, Lester, David, and DeMouse, are trying to waylay in Springfield." Grandpa paused. He glanced at GFF perched on Thomas's bed staring out the window and continued, "A watchdog not bigger than a minute who can't protect himself, and tattooed hoodlums trying to rob our fireworks tent. Now we've got Sydney bringing a wizard woman who thinks we've got spirits! We're supposed to be operating a business."

Thomas resolutely closed his laptop. "Are you thinking what I'm thinking, Grandpa?"

"What's that?" Grandpa muttered, causing GFF to turn briefly away from his post at the window.

"I'm thinking we made a promise to run this fireworks tent. Something or somebody is doing their best to cause us to break that promise. I'm not backing down! Come heat, robbers, spooks, or stalkers, we owe TNT that much." Thomas reached over to pat GFF. "Guard the camper, General Freddie Freedom! Me and Grandpa have got to go to work."

Chapter 12

Hero

As the end of June approached, bringing with it the last weekend before the Fourth of July, Sunday customers were as demanding as the sun beating down on the vinyl fireworks tent.

"Grandpa, you think it's too hot for Harley?" Thomas looked at their landlord lounging in a deck chair in the shade of the awning of the camper. GFF was sprawled on the grass near him.

"I should be so cool." Grandpa mopped the sweat from his face with his bandana as he sacked fireworks, "You better restock the assortment bags."

"Young man," a deep voice called from near the entrance, "can you help me and my friend with some fireworks?"

"Sydney!" Thomas left his post behind the counter and ran to greet his friend Ahunk, Sydney Snyder, with a welcoming hug.

Sydney returned the greeting. Then, he held Thomas at arms' length surveying his friend. "You're taller." He grasped the boy's biceps and squeezed. "Are those real muscles?"

Thomas laughed. "Just wait till you start lugging these cases. You'll have muscles, too."

Sydney punched Thomas's arm in a playful gesture. "Thomas, this is Kaylene!" Beside him stood a beautifully tanned young woman in a tank top and shorts. She had the blackest hair

Thomas had ever seen.

"Hello." Kaylene's clear blue eyes twinkled to a warm gray.

"Thomas," Grandpa hollered, "you and Sydney bring that pretty girl in here and help me."

Sydney was soon helping Grandpa check out customers while Thomas restocked shelves. Trying to keep cool, Kaylene pulled her long hair up and twisted it into a coil on top of her head.   She kept watching Harley, who sat like royalty on his lawn chair throne and chatted with many of the older people. Finally, she said, "I'm going to join the man in the lawn chair by the dog."

Thomas called,"Harley, meet Kaylene from California. She and Sydney are going to help us for the rest of the season."

Several of the customers yelled, "Hey, Kaylene. Hey, Sydney."

The Californians played to their audience, waving as though they were in a parade.

Harley motioned Kaylene to an empty lawn chair. GFF was straining at his lease wagging his body with pleasure. Kaylene leaned down to gather him up in a hug.

"That's the man who owns the property, right?" Sydney asked.

Grandpa nodded. "I hope she doesn't let on that she knows about his sons and the dog disappearing."

"Don't worry about Kaylene. She'll have Harley wrapped around her little finger before he knows what happened." Sydney smiled like he was speaking from experience.

"She's already got GFF drooling," Thomas said.

At noon Martin and Wendy arrived lugging fast food bags.

"You hungry? Need some help?" Wendy called as she and her dad joined the others behind the counter.

"Mom wanted to come but Dad thought it would be too hot," Wendy whispered to Thomas as she passed out baskets to customers.

Thomas nodded and hurried to open another case of bottle rockets.

The crowd thickened considerably as church services let out.

"Yip, yip-yip!" GFF strained at his lease trying to get to Harley and Kaylene who were returning from a tour of the barn.

"Grandpa, do you think GFF is all right? Should I untie him and bring him in here?" Thomas asked.

"A dog under foot is the last thing we need. It's plenty hot in here, too." Grandpa pulled his bandana from his pocket and tied it around his head like a head band, stopping the sweat from running into his eyes. "Speaking of things underfoot, what's that little kid doing behind the counter?" Grandpa asked.

"I'll take her back to her mother, again." Thomas reached for the toddler in red overalls. "Her name is Susie." Thomas leaned closer to Grandpa, "I think Susie is going to have a new brother or sister before long." He nodded toward two women, one in maternity clothes.

"Well, they better hang on to the kid. She'll get lost in this crowd," Grandpa said. "After you return the kid, go to the storage trailer and bring in a case of colored smoke balls."

After delivering Susie to her mom, Thomas stopped to pet GFF and talk to Kaylene and Harley. Behind the camper, he crawled into the trailer and rearranged cases to get to the smoke balls. As he started back, the squeal of tires caused him to turn toward the highway where another car had slowed to turn in the driveway. A flash of red close to the road caught his attention.

"Thomas, hurry up with those smoke bombs!" Grandpa called.

Thomas headed toward the side entrance of the tent.

"Susie! Has anyone seen my little girl?" It was the pregnant woman. She was just coming out of the tent with the other woman close behind.

"Ruth, please. You're getting too hot. Sit here." Her friend motioned to a cluster of lawn chairs. "I'll look for Susie. She's probably inside pestering that boy again."

"No ma'am." Thomas called, "I'm out here but I'll help you look for Susie." He remembered the cute little girl in red overalls.

Red Overalls! He'd seen a flash of red near the road. Surely, it couldn't have been the toddler.

Thomas deposited the cases of smoke balls inside the tent and ran toward the road calling, "Susie, Susie!"

He heard a high pitched voice shrilling, "Mama, Mama."

His heart skipped a beat when he saw the little girl headed toward the busy highway.

He heard the other woman's scream and knew she had seen the girl, too.

"What is it? Where is my baby?" The mother was up and running toward them.

Thomas was closest. He ran toward Susie calling her name.

She turned and saw him. Giggling, she began to run again.

"Susieeeeee!" The mother's screech told Thomas she had seen her child.

Hearing her mother's voice the little girl hesitated, turning toward the sound. She was on the shoulder of the highway poised to move into the traffic as Thomas reached out and grabbed her red overall strap. He jerked her backwards into his arms.

"Honk! Honk!" Horns blared as Thomas stood near the side of the road hugging the small body to him.

"Susie!" The other woman reached for the child. Thomas handed her over reluctantly.

"My baby! Susie, are you okay, honey?" The mother grabbed the child from her friend.

"Ruth, are you all right? You look worse than Susie." The other woman put a hand on her friend's shoulder. "Let's get out of this heat." They turned toward the tent.

Thomas followed close behind hoping they wouldn't turn the child loose again.

Suddenly a whoop went up from the crowd outside the fireworks tent. They applauded the child's safety and the boy who'd saved her.

Martin ran to Thomas. "Are you okay?"

Wendy was close behind, "You're a hero, Thomas!" She turned to the cheering crowd and yelled, "Thomas is my big brother."

"Thomas, Thomas!" the crowd repeated his name.

The two women turned as if embarrassed they hadn't acknowledged the boy's efforts.

The mother walked toward him holding Susie's hand tightly. "Thanks for saving my daughter." She extended her hand toward him.

As Thomas reached to take her hand, she slumped to the ground.

"Mama, Mama!" Susie cried.

Her friend rushed forward. "Ruth! Is it the baby?"

The mother's hands were gripping her stomach. She began to scream.

"Thomas, run to the tent. Call nine-one-one. Get an ambulance here, fast." Martin turned to his daughter. "Wendy, hold on to the little girl."

Thoughts raced through Thomas's mind as he ran to the tent. Was Susie's mother going to have her baby now?

The shrill scream of a siren eased traffic to the side of the road. An ambulance pulled into the drive. Not far behind was a television van.

Martin stood near the road entrance. He waved the emergency vehicle to where Sydney stood waiting with Thomas and the two women. Wendy held Susie's hand talking gently to her.

Paramedics jumped to the ground almost before the ambulance stopped. They examined the mother quickly. Two men moved forward with a stretcher and loaded the mother in the back. Her friend and Susie crawled in their car to follow. The siren whined a wail of alert and moved onto the highway.

Nearby, a man with a big camera on his shoulder focused on a woman talking into a microphone, "This is Stella Stiles reporting live from Branson, Missouri, where a few minutes ago a young girl was saved by a brave young man working at this fireworks tent on the Harley Jones farm." She paused to let the camera sweep over the fireworks tent. "The Fourth of July is only four days away and cars jam the parking lot as people shop for fireworks to celebrate Independence Day . . . "

Thomas gawked at the scene until another man motioned him and Wendy over to where Stella stood.

"My brother is a hero!" Wendy told Stella, "His name is Thomas Scott."

Stella's eyes brightened recognizing a name recently in the news. She ad-libbed, "Acts of heroism are no stranger to Thomas Scott. Less than two weeks ago this young man stood on the stage at Ozark, Missouri . . . " Stella motioned Thomas to stand beside her as she interviewed him.

Martin approached Stella. "I'd rather you

didn't run this boy's picture on televison." They had a hurried consultation. Thomas heard Martin say, ". . . put the boy in danger."

"Oh my gosh!" Thomas capped a hand over his mouth. If the story made the news Jervis would see it.

Martin led Thomas and Wendy back to the tent. "Let's get back inside and help Grandpa. He and Sydney are swamped. We'll talk about this later."

"But, the mother? Is her baby going to be okay, Daddy?" Wendy's eyes filled with tears.

"Yes, darling. She was lucky a hospital was so close. We'll call later and see if everything is all right."

"Dad," Wendy asked,"Mom and our baby won't have any trouble will they?"

Martin put an arm around Wendy and Thomas. "Mom is going to be just fine. That's why she's at home and not out here in this heat."

People had gathered outside the tent to watch the excitement but many still prowled the tables loaded with fireworks. Soon Martin was helping Grandpa and Sydney take money and sack purchases while Wendy and Thomas helped customers.

Grandpa handed Thomas a roll of paper. "Put these NO SMOKING signs up at every entrance. "You'd think people would be smart enough to know not to smoke in or near a fireworks stand."

"Look at Kaylene!" Sydney hollered. "The front parking area is full and Harley and her are opening the meadow for parking."

Kaylene stood near the camper directing cars behind the tent. Harley sat near GFF shouting instruction to her.

"Thomas Scott!"

Thomas looked up and blinked his eyes as a flash bulb went off. It was a reporter who had interviewed him at Ozark during the award ceremony. The man waved a 'thank you' gesture.

"Stop!" Martin called after him.

Screams erupted from the area behind the tent. Recognizing Kaylene's voice, Sydney pushed through the crowd to the side entrance and raced outside.

"Help!" Harley's voice was hoarse with fear. GFF's yip mirrored Harley's cries.

Thomas searched the meadow for Kaylene. And, then he saw the reason for the screams. A plume of smoke drifted skyward near the farthest row of cars.

"Fire!" Thomas shouted as he grabbed a fire extinguisher and dashed from the tent. He wove among the cars until he broke free into the clearing where Sydney and Kaylene stomped burning grass.

"Help!" Thomas urged a customer who stood gawking. "Squelch it!"

As if waking from a trance, customers ran forward and joined the stomping until it looked like they were preforming an Indian rain dance.

A man came running with an ice chest and dumped it over the area. The flames sucked the ice greedily choking on it's moisture.

Thomas activated the fire extinguisher and

foamed the edges of the fire before it could spread farther.

A flash flicking caused Thomas to turn quickly, fire extinguisher extended to splash another outbreak.

"Hold it!" The man with the camera shouted flashing another picture.

"Don't—" Thomas yelled as the man moved into the crowd and disappeared.

The damage was confined to a small area of the meadow. Cars exited the back field. The excitement wore off quickly. Helpers returned to the tent, sweat stained and streaked with smoke.

"Good work, crew!" Grandpa praised. "I wonder what started the fire?"

Thomas held up a sooty hand. Pinched between two fingers was the remains of a partially stubbed-out cigarette.

Chapter 13
Where's Jervis?

The first day of July was a scorcher.

"You made the news, Wonderman!" Sydney yelled, when he and Kaylene arrived. He jumped out of the car holding a copy of a newspaper. "And, the weatherman says there's a weather front moving in that might bring rain!"

"Did you hear that, Grandpa? If it rains maybe it'll get cooler."

"And, maybe we'll sell more fireworks because folks won't be afraid to shoot them when it's so dry," Grandpa said. "You're joking about Thomas being in the news, right?"

Kaylene waved as she pulled the car around the tent and drove up the lane to Harley's house.

GFF ran the length of his leash barking.

"Sorry GFF. Looks like we've lost our gal to Farmer Jones," Sydney said. "And, yes, rain is a possibility. And, there is a story about Thomas in the newspaper. I'll show you as soon as we get the side curtains rolled up." He laid the newspaper on the counter and continued talking as he helped Grandpa and Thomas, "Kaylene and Harley went to his house yesterday after the fire. While they were talking, Harley told her about his missing boys and Booger, the missing dog."

"Was it pretty much what he told us?" Grandpa asked.

Sydney nodded. "She said they are developing a kinship. She believes her extrasensory perception can link them with the turbulent spirits, who seem to habitant the woods and cemetery."

"I hope she doesn't get Harley all shook up over this nonsense," Grandpa grumbled.

"I wonder if she told Harley she thinks the turbulent spirits are a huge dog and a young boy?" Thomas asked.

Sydney shook his head. "She doesn't think he is quite ready for that. At any rate he agreed to walk with her to the cemetery. He thinks someone has been messing around the caretaker's shed back there."

"With everything that's been going on around here, they better not go back there by themselves. Let's call security and have them check it out," Grandpa said.

"Good idea, I'll run up and tell them as soon as we get open. Meanwhile . . ." He smoothed out the newspaper and began to read, "Whether Thomas Scott is putting out a grass fire or saving a young child's life, it's all in a day's work."

"You weren't joking?" Grandpa leaned over the counter, adjusted his glasses, and reached for the newspaper. He read, "Although No Smoking signs are posted on the grounds of Scott's tent on the Harley Jones Farm near Branson, customers seem to pay little attention." Grandpa hooted. "He's got that right!"

Sydney pointed to the next paragraph. "Quick thinking on the part of young Thomas added another notch to his hero belt."

"No way!" Thomas said, "you are making that up."

Sydney shook his head, and continued, "When a customer's partially stubbed-out cigarette ignited dry grass behind the fireworks tent, Thomas quickly controlled the blaze with his fire extinguisher."

Grandpa scoffed, "Hummp! Some blaze! Kaylene had so many customers stomping out that bit of fire it looked like they were preforming an Indian rain dance."

"Someone dumped a cooler of ice over the fire just before I got there with the extinguisher," Thomas said.

"Hey! There's more, Wonderman." Sydney read on, "Fans of young Scott were quick to point out he saved a child from running onto the highway. The girl's mother was experiencing premature labor. Thomas alerted nine-one-one, who transported the woman to the hospital where she delivered a baby boy."

"A brother for Susie!" Thomas beamed.

"Maybe they'll name him Thomas or WONDERMAN after the boy hero." Grandpa chuckled.

"Very funny, Grandpa!" Thomas laughed, but the laughter died in this throat as he glimpsed the picture the photojournalist had snapped of him.

"You and the fireworks tent are plastered across the front page of the Springfield newspaper, boy hero. This publicity might be good for business but you can bet you-know-who will see it, too," Grandpa muttered.

"Jervis!" Thomas said, "I wonder if Martin has seen this?"

"Ringggg," Grandpa's cell phone announced a caller. He glanced at the caller ID. "Hello, Martin." He listened. "Yes, we've seen the paper." Grandpa listened. His eyes darted from Thomas to Sydney. Then, he exclaimed, "What? Both of them? Cleared out completely?"

"What, Grandpa?"

Grandpa put a finger to his lips to silence Thomas. "We'll be alert." He paused. "Yes, he's right here." Grandpa handed Thomas the phone.

"What's going on?" Thomas asked Martin. His eyes widened as he listened. "Did they go in and check it out?" Thomas asked.

It was Grandpa's turn to question, "What?"

Thomas shook his head and continued to listen. "Everything was gone?" Thomas asked. He listened for a long time nodding and shaking his head in silence communication. "Wow!" Thomas exclaimed, "Sure, Martin. I'll tell them. We'll see you soon." Thomas handed the phone back to Grandpa, who immediately raised his eyebrows in question.

"Martin said Jervis's son must have come back yesterday. Neighbors were complaining about the yelling and banging next door. They thought he might be beating his kid, again."

"Were they still watching the house or did the neighbor call the police?" Sydney asked.

"Both, Lester and Pappy were watching and called Martin. Martin's buddy at the Sheriff's Department got a search warrant and they went in this morning."

"What. . .?" Grandpa began.

Thomas continued, "Jervis, the kid, the pickup, and dogs, were gone. The house was deserted. But. . ." Thomas hesitated.

"Well. . ." Grandpa glanced at Sydney frowning.

"What did they find?" Sydney asked.

"A suitcase filled with newspaper clippings, medical papers, and old bottles of medicine. Jervis was hospitalized and under treatment of a psychiatrist for months." Thomas gulped.

Grandpa rubbed his chin. "So, Jervis is a nutcase?"

"It seems he was being treated for severe depression after he, his wife, Molly, and son, Roy, were in involved in a car accident."

"Where's his wife?" Sydney asked.

"She died in the car accident. One of his neighbors said Jervis blamed himself for her death because he was driving," Thomas said.

"What about Roy, his son?" Sydney asked.

"That's the weird thing. The neighbor said Roy's dog caused the accident. He got away from the boy and jumped onto Jervis causing him to swerve into the path of an oncoming semi."

"Was Roy hurt?" Sydney asked.

"Martin said the newspaper story said Jervis was the only survivor of the accident."

"So, who was the boy with Jervis the night of the party?" Grandpa asked. "Who was the kid who ran away and came back? Who was Jervis yelling at when the neighbor overheard him?"

Thomas shook his head. "Who knows? Do you think that's why he treats dogs so mean? If he blames his son he must blame the dog, too?"

"Martin said they are headed down here," Thomas said.

"Jervis and his son!" Grandpa gasped.

"No, no! Martin was on his cell phone. He and Wendy are on their way. Lester, David, and Pappy are right behind them. They are worried about us." Thomas sighed. "They think Jervis is still hunting for me. Well, we'll just be open three more days?"

"Four, counting today. We've got the biggest days of fireworks sales coming up and a stalker on the loose. Besides . . . " Grandpa stopped as a car pulled in the drive. He looked at Thomas, "There's something else, isn't there? You look green around the gills."

"Martin said someone cut the picture of WONDERMAN off a fireworks label and tacked it to Jervis's wall. Across the warrior's body was scrawled in red pencil, THOMAS SCOTT! DOGS!"

Grandpa shuddered. "So, it was him and his son who stole the WONDERMAN shell?"

Thomas nodded. "And, maybe he is still hunting for me and GFF." Thomas took a deep breath and squared his shoulders, "But, you know what?" Thomas watched kids unload from a car and head toward the tent. "Right now, we've got customers! And, security is as close as our alarm button."

"You're right, boy! Time to go to work. Martin and the others will be here soon."

Sydney patted Thomas on the shoulder. "Stay close to your Grandpa. I'm going to run up and tell Kaylene and Harley to stay close to the house. We'll have security check out that shed. Be right back."

Thomas began to restock. He mused," So, Jervis and his son still have a WONDERMAN shell? Wonder how many loads they have left? We know they shot part of their ZEUS fire-crackers at Ozark. They are going to run out of ammo soon. Then what?"

"We'll worry about that when the time comes," Grandpa said. "By then, we'll have more help. And, like you said, we've got security close." He handed a basket to a customer and pointed out the prices.

"Wendy's coming too. Martin said Lester and Pappy would go back to Springfield nights and check with the police on Jervis. He and Wendy are going to stay at your cabin."

Grandpa nodded. "We'll probably need them all before the Fourth is over."

"Martin said David would like to bunk here with us. What do you think?" Thomas asked.

Grandpa nodded.

"Ringggg!" Thomas's cell phone buzzed. He checked the caller ID. NO CALLER IDENTIFI-CATION the green light announced.

"Grandpa!" Thomas said, holding out his phone.

"Hello, who is this?" Grandpa bellowed into the receiver.

"Thomas, er, Tom, I tried your phone and it was busy!" Sydney shouted, "We've called nine-one-one! Harley needs help!"

Once more sirens screamed a path to the fireworks tent. This time they drove on to Harley's farm house. Just as quickly they returned and sped toward the hospital, sirens still shrilling.

"I'm glad Kaylene rode to the hospital with Harley," Thomas said.

"I told her I'd pick her up after we close tonight. Everyone else will be here by then." Sydney said.

"Do you think Harley will be okay?" Thomas asked.

"According to the paramedics his heart was acting up. I guess the excitement and heat were too much for him yesterday. They called his doctor. He's going to meet them at the hospital and check him over."

"Thomas!" Wendy ran into the tent with Martin behind her. "Are you okay? Dad and I met the ambulance pulling out. We were afraid Jervis . . . "

"Slow down, Wendy," Martin said. "It looks like everyone is okay. So, who was in the ambulance?"

As they waited on customers, Grandpa, Sydney, and Thomas, filled Martin and Wendy in on the morning's events.

People crowded the aisles pushing to fill their baskets. Thomas raced around trying to keep the counters restocked.

"Look at the cool Land Rover!" Thomas said,

as a vehicle resembling an army car pulled up to the camper. Three men climbed out.

"Hey, it's David, his dad, and Pappy DeMouse!" Thomas said.

David waved and motioned to the barn.

Thomas gave him a 'thumbs up' signal and watched as they began walking through the grass toward the barn. Later, when the crowd had thinned, they returned.

"Need help, Thomas?" David followed Lester and Pappy behind the counter.

"Here, David, grab this case." Thomas paused, a question in his eye, remembering how concerned Lester was for his son.

Lester nodded, and David lifted the case easily onto the counter. The boys begin filling empty spaces.

"David told me about that barn but I found it hard to believe," Pappy said.

Lester kept up a running conversation with Martin and Sydney as they showed them around the tent.

"Dad? Are you going to tell them about Daisy and the dogs at the shelter?" David asked.

"Oh, yes! We stopped by the shelter to tell Daisy we would be out of town until after the Fourth." He paused, as Grandpa made change for a customer. Then, he continued, "Daisy said Jervis broke into the shelter. He brought back the dogs and his keys. The night security video caught him on film. She played it for us."

David said, "He didn't turn on the lights in the office so the quality was poor. We couldn't see his son or his wife but he was talking to them."

"Stop! Hold on!" Thomas turned away from the counter where he was restocking cones, "His wife? His son? I thought they both died in the car accident? Do you think he remarried? Did his new wife have a son?"

"Thomas! Stop speculating and let them tell their story," Grandpa said.

"We saw Jervis open the drawer where the keys are kept to return the one he had." Lester said.

"Why . . . ?" Thomas began and stopped as Grandpa gave him a look.

"The weird part was the argument they were all having," David said. "Jervis said he kept his promise and the boy better keep his or he'd be sorry."

Lester shook his head, "Weird is a good word for it. Like David said, we couldn't see the boy but we heard him. The boy said, 'Dad, you only kept part of your promise by returning the dogs. So, I'll only keep part of my promise to bring back Mom.'"

"Bring back his mother! She's dead, unless . . ." Thomas looked at Grandpa, "I'm sorry but I think Jervis and his whole family is nuts."

"I'm with you, Thomas," David said. "At the end, Jervis yelled, 'Molly!'"

"We heard a woman's voice say, 'Jervis, I can't stay but I'll be back. If you hurt our son again I'm going to take you with me when I go.'" David shivered.

"Then Jervis lunged toward the camera

screaming, 'Molly, come back!' And, the screen went black," Lester finished.

"Will Daisy let us use that tape for evidence?" Martin asked.

"I had her call the Sheriff's office. They are coming by to pick it up. They are going to send it to the doctor who treated Jervis to see if he can help. They are alerting the Branson police to watch for his pickup."

Pappy was silent and withdrawn throughout the report. He kept looking toward the farm house. When Lester finished, he spoke, "Do Harley Jones and his wife still live in the farm house?"

As Grandpa made change, he answered, "Harley's wife died not long after he lost his sons."

"Died? Lost his sons?" Pappy echoed.

Thomas nodded. "This morning Harley got sick and they took him to the hospital."

Pappy echoed, " . . . took Harley to the hospital?"

Lester came over to stand behind Pappy. "Dad, are you okay? You look pale."

Pappy nodded. "Why don't you start at the beginning and tell me about Harley, his boys, and what happened to cause him to go to the hospital."

While Grandpa waited on customers, Thomas continued the story. The others helped with the fireworks but Pappy slumped on a case of bottle rockets listening to the tale.

"So, he believes both Mick and Dave are dead?" Pappy asked.

Thomas hesitated, he didn't remember saying the missing boys' names. Had Pappy noticed them on the picture mounted on the well? Slowly, he continued, "Harley told me and Grandpa he kept the barn fixed up hoping one day his boys would return, but I think he's beginning to believe they are never coming back."

Pappy wandered out to the lawn chair near GFF. Later, he returned with colas for everyone. He said he was going to drive around and check out the changes in his old hometown.

"That's right. Your hometown is Branson," Thomas said, "You told the reporter at Ozark Branson was a hilly, curvy road."

"From what I've seen so far Branson's still hilly and curvy but the roads are a lot better." Pappy said as he headed for the Land Rover.

Something Pappy said was so familiar it bothered Thomas. He thought about it as customers filled their baskets, left, and were replaced by others. Finally, he stopped worrying about it.

The boys kept restocking. The men set up another check-out counter. Wendy retrieved baskets from the checkout and returned them to the entrance.

It was late afternoon when Pappy returned. Thomas glimpsed him walking past the old barn toward the woods leading to the cemetery. "Do you think your grandpa is lost?" Thomas asked David.

David followed Thomas's gaze and saw Pappy disappear into the trees at the back of

Harley's farm. "No, he likes to walk. When we went to the barn he mentioned going to the old cemetery and looking at the river."

"How did he know . . .?"

"Ya-room!" Near the east end of Harley's farm an artillery shell blasted into the sky. The crowd paused to watch the show.

"Do you think someone's shooting fireworks on Harley's land, Grandpa? We promised him . . ." Thomas said.

An older man who had been to the tent before and visited with Harley said, "I don't think whoever's shooting those fireworks is on Harley's land. There's an old dirt maintenance road over there. Four wheelers have just about taken it over." The old man paused, "Trouble is, they're aiming the fireworks this way and they're landing on Harley. Dry as it is . . . "

"I'll go have a look," Martin said, "Thomas, why don't you come with me? Get GFF and bring him along. Wendy, you stay in the tent!"

The turn-off to the dirt road was overgrown with low trees and bushes.

"There it is!" Thomas pointed just as Martin put his signal light on.

"This is nothing more than a glorified cow path," Martin said, trying to steer over the ruts.

Thomas pointed to the sky. "There! Another shell just went off. They're still shooting."

Martin edged around a tight turn and saw some kids on four wheelers parked ahead. He honked to get their attention and pulled up behind them. Several of the boys continued to watch the fireworks. One boy reluctantly broke away and came over to Martin's vehicle.

"You boys realize your fireworks are going onto Harley Jones farm? His pasture is really dry and . . ." Martin admonished.

"Not us, man! We aren't shooting. We're just watching," the boy protested.

"Do you know who's shooting?" Martin asked.

"Some dude up the road. We stopped to watch and he run us off. Said we were bothering his wife and boy."

"Sorry, we'll go talk to him," Martin said.

"No sweat! Be careful, he's a nut case." The boy started back to his group, then turned. "Hey, aren't you the kid who runs that fireworks tent? I saw your picture . . ." He stopped when Thomas nodded.

"Yes, the man we rent from doesn't want any fireworks shot on his land," Thomas said.

"Tell it to the dude in the green pickup. Man, I can't wait to tell my friends I met Thomas Scott!" The kid ran toward his friends who were starting back to their bikes.

"Green pickup!" Thomas and Martin said at the same time.

Martin gunned his motor to life.

The kid yelled, "You better hurry! The dude's leaving."

Chapter 14
A Hero's Story

"How did you and Martin lose Jervis?" David asked Thomas as they helped themselves to a hotdog from supplies Pappy deposited on the table in front of the camper.

Martin, Sydney, and Lester, were helping Grandpa roll the side curtains down and Wendy was collecting baskets. A last minute customer pulled up and ran inside the tent.

"We chased that green pickup around curves bouncing over ruts and ditches. It was like a maze. Suddenly, we came out to the highway. Jervis and whoever was with him were gone."

"Probably cut through the back of Harley's land," said Pappy. "There's an old maintenance road that winds down the cliff to the river. It continues to the back of the farm."

"Wow!" Thomas said, "Pappy, you must have walked all over Harley's farm. Did you see a shed? Harley thought someone was messing around back there."

Pappy squinted at the dark hulk of the barn behind them. "I walked miles on this farm. I believe I know it like it was my own."

David coughed, almost choking on his hotdog. Pappy got up and slapped him on the back. He spoke softly to him until David straightened up, shook his head, and grinned sheepishly.

"And, Thomas, I didn't get as far as the shed Harley uses as a garage. I might check it out tomorrow and be sure his tools are safe," Pappy said.

"Who told you Harley has tools there?" Thomas waited for Pappy to answer, but he must not have heard the question. Thomas continued, "Grandpa was going to have Martin call security but it got so hectic today I bet they forgot."

Suddenly a voice boomed, "You're surrounded. Give it up! Last warning before we shoot!"

"What the . . ." Pappy yelled.

Light flooded the tent and the image of the huge Black Cat appeared against the yellow and red vinyl near the center pole. A shrill "Meowwwwwwww" echoed through the darkness as the image of a Black Cat screamed.

"Yowlllllllll!" An answering cry came from the woods and moved forward toward the barn.

David shivered. "What was that?"

GFF growled and hunkered closer to Thomas.

Voices sounded from the tent as the men and Wendy emerged with the customer. The tent lights went out. The glow of flashlights walked toward the camper.

"It sounds like Grandpa pushed the security button by mistake. Now, we won't have to call security. They'll be on their way." Thomas picked up GFF who was trying to climb his leg. "But, the other noise may have been the big cat who prowled around here when we first set up."

Grandpa, Sydney, Martin, Wendy, and Lester moved into the circle of light.

"You think the cat's back, Grandpa?" Thomas asked.

Before Grandpa could answer, Pappy nodded toward the barn, "That's no cat. It's a big dog!"

"You're right, Pappy," Sydney said. "At least that's what the image maker CD Thomas sent me revealed. Kaylene says it's a huge dog. There was a blurry shadow behind it that appeared to be a young boy."

"Kaylene is a nice girl but she's sensitive. Isn't that what they call it, Sydney?" Grandpa asked helping himself to a sandwich.

Sydney nodded. "Speaking of Kaylene, I better get to the hospital and pick her up. She's been with Harley all day."

"Take care of that black-haired beauty, Sydney," Pappy said as Sydney left.

Thomas stared at Pappy, wondering how he knew Kayleen's hair was black. He was beginning to wonder a lot about Pappy.

"Yowlllllllll!" The cry sounded closer.

"Yes sir! It's the big dog," Pappy muttered.

Lester put a hand on his father's shoulder. "Dad . . . ?"

"Why don't you get something to eat, Lester," Pappy said, "I've got a story to tell."

Sirens sounded in the distance and came closer. A car with red light whirling atop skidded to a stop near the entrance of the tent. Two men jumped out.

Grandpa yelled, "False alarm!"

The men cut the siren and walked over to the group.

"Sorry," Grandpa said sheepishly, "I hit the wrong button."

"Grab a sandwich," Martin said. While everyone helped themselves to food, Martin brought the security men up-to-date on Jervis. He mentioned Harley was in the hospital and wanted them to check the shed behind his house.

"I'd be glad to take you down there tomorrow, gentlemen. I was planning on checking the machine shed myself," Pappy said.

The security men turned to look at Pappy.

"This is Pappy DeMouse," Thomas said. "He's a hero from World War Two. He shot down nineteen aces. He's been walking the farm today. He knows where the shed is located."

Pappy extended his hand to the men. "Sit down boys. I was just fixing to tell a story. You might find it interesting, too."

"Might as well," the security man said. "All we got tonight is a false alarm and notice to watch this area for a green pickup."

His partner interrupted, "Hey, remember the CD Thomas copied for us? The one of the huge image behind the little dog?"

"Did you get a report back from your lab?" Thomas asked.

"Strangest thing. They confirmed the oversized image was that of a dog. The blurry outline behind it was what they believe is the image of a boy. Does that make sense?"

"Only that Kaylene may be more sensitive than we know, right Grandpa?" Thomas winked at Martin.

"Still don't make sense to me," Grandpa grumbled. "Pappy, didn't you say you had a story to tell?"

They settled down to listen to the war hero's story.

"Thomas, you remember the other night when we were talking about gangsters and you asked me if I really met Elliot Ness?"

Thomas nodded. "Did you?"

"Yes, he was one of the good guys. I knew him because of the bad crowd I ran with when I was a young man. Most of the big, bad names were gone by then but Alvin Karpis lingered on. He served time in Alcatraz." Pappy's voice was husky as he continued, "When he went up, we knew even the biggest of the bad guys could get caught and serve time." Pappy sank into a chair like a deflated balloon. "I'd had my share of trouble. I wanted to make up for it. When Pearl Harbor shook the world, I decided to join the air force."

"Are you sure you want to do this, Dad?" Lester asked.

"Got to, son."

"So, you joined the Air Force and that's when you started shooting down planes?" Thomas asked.

"Not so fast," Pappy said, "the Air Force wasn't letting any Mickey Mouse jump in a plane and start shooting. I was a mechanic, of sorts."

Pappy's mention of Mickey Mouse made Thomas remember the story Harley told them that first day about his son, Mick, being a mechanic. "Did you work on car engines, Pappy?"

The old man's face looked weary in the lamplight. He nodded and continued, "They taught me how to work on plane engines as I trained to fly. One day they thought this Mickey Mouse was ready to fly."

"Mickey Mouse!" Thomas mumbled, "Mick . . ." It was all beginning to come together.

"Tell them how you got your name, Pappy." David said proudly.

"I was no stranger to death. Now, I flew into its face everyday. I took with me the memory of death." Pappy's eye grew sad. "I thought of death as the big D. When I got an enemy plane in my sights, just before I pulled the trigger, I'd say, 'This one's for you, D.' So, my aces were listed as D-1, D-2, and so on. The guys in my company put the handle 'Mickey Mouse' together with D and began calling me DeMouse. Pappy was an honorary name, of sorts."

Thomas stared at Pappy wide-eyed realizing what he had just told them. But, he had to be sure. "What did the D stand for, Pappy? Could it be Dave?"

Pappy nodded. "You're a smart boy, Thomas. Yes, the big D for me was the memory of the death of my brother, Dave."

"You shot all those planes down in your brother's name?" Thomas asked.

Again Pappy nodded, and said, "My brother died before he had a chance to experience life. In a way, it was like he was there with me shooting down the enemy. Together, we were making the world a better place to live for our mom and dad and all the folks back home."

Thomas gasped, "Grandpa! It's . . . "

Grandpa's eyes brimmed with tears. He reached toward Pappy and uttered one word, "Mick?"

Thomas looked at Martin, who nodded understanding.

Lester and David stood beside Pappy, Mick DeMouse, whose brother Dave had disappeared along with Mick and the big dog, Booger, so many years ago. Now, Mick had returned to explain what happened that day.

Pappy's eyes were bright with tears. "I promised Lester's wife, just before she died, I would return and make things right so my ma and pa could meet their grandson, Lester, and their great-grandson, David."

"Mick Jones! I can't believe it's you." Grandpa exclaimed, "I used to come to your house to play basketball with my brother, Bud."

Pappy nodded. "I figured that out, Tom. I told Lester and David if anyone might recognize me it would be you. But, it's been a lot of years. We were both a lot younger." Pappy stretched out a hand.

Grandpa rose, walked to Pappy and shook his hand. "It's good to see you, Mick."

"My gosh!" Thomas exclaimed. "Wait until

Harley realizes his son is home."

"That's what's bothering me. When we came down here I was ready to tell him. Then, I learned Ma was dead," Pappy stammered. "And, Pa was in the hospital. Now, I'm afraid the shock will be too much for him."

Thomas was piecing the story together. "So, you moved to Springfield with Lester and David hoping to find a way to get them together with Harley?"

"That's right." Lester answered for his dad. "When you and Martin walked into the animal shelter that day it was like a prayer had been answered.

"But, we couldn't do anything until Pappy decided it was time," David said. "I came down here and played basketball with my great-grandfather in the barn where everything happened. I couldn't wait to tell Pappy."

"Then, we got in the middle of this Jervis situation," Pappy said. "Danger was everywhere. It was like someone was telling me to get my planes in a row before it was too late. I was afraid he'd die before I could make it right." Pappy's voice broke. "I stopped at the hospital today while I was in town. I met Kaylene."

"So, that's how you knew she had black hair!" Thomas said.

Pappy nodded. "She figured out who I was when I tried to explain to the nurses I was kin to the old man." Pappy sighed. "I told her the whole story."

"Wait until she tells Sydney. He'll never forgive himself for missing your story, Pappy,"

Thomas said.

"The story's not over, Thomas. Harley still doesn't know. I don't know if he'll believe this old man," he gestured at himself, "is his oldest son who disappeared so many years ago. To him, I'm as dead as Dave."

"You'll find a way, Pappy. We'll help you. It's like a miracle, isn't it, Grandpa?"

The security men glanced around the group trying to understand what was happening.

"Thomas, why is everyone crying?" Wendy asked as she moved closer to her dad. "Is this really one of the missing boys? What happened to the other one? And, what happened to the big, black, dog, Booger?"

"I believe they are crying for a hero who has come home to bury his brother and a dog named—" Thomas stopped as a loud growl pierced the air.

"Booger!" Pappy shouted.

Chapter 15
Discovery

A huge shadow loomed against the outline of the tent.

"Yowlllllllll!" screamed the shadow.

"Yip, yip-yip!" challenged GFF as he tried to crawl beneath Thomas's shirt.

"Quick, everyone, into the camper," Grandpa yelled.

Everyone scrambled toward the camper. The security men dove for their vehicle parked nearby.

Inside Thomas raced for his laptop and accessed the security software just as the camper swayed as though a strong wind had whipped against it. In the distance the rumble of thunder resounded.

"Yowlllllllll!" The cry surrounded them.

"Do something, Thomas!" Grandpa shouted, "What was it you did before?"

"I'm trying." Thomas's commanded his fingers to type. He pressed ENTER and the tent outside lit up like a circus. His fingers moved again and he pressed ENTER. The image of a huge Black Cat appeared on the red and yellow vinyl near the top of the tent. It was shrieking.

"Look out the window, Martin," Thomas said. "Do you see anything?"

"Just lightning in the distance," Martin said, reaching for a handhold on the cabinet as the camper swayed from another blow.

"Do something, Thomas!" Wendy pleaded. "Don't let it get me."

"Be still, little lady," Pappy said starting toward the door. "It's not you it's after, it's me. I don't think it'll rest until it's tasted death. I may have to face it before I see my dad."

"Wait, Pappy!" Thomas said. "If it doesn't fear the cat maybe it'll fear itself. When I push SEND, this time, I want you to yell, 'fetch' just like you did that day, remember?"

Pappy nodded and moved to the small microphone attached to the laptop.

"Let me do it, Pappy," David said.

Pappy nodded and handed his grandson the microphone.

Again Thomas's fingers did their work. He glanced at David and nodded as he pushed ENTER.

"Fetch! Booger, fetch!" David commanded.

The software projected the humongous shadow of a big dog. It loomed against the background of the tent.

Thomas watched out the camper window as the aggressive twin shadow edged toward its image highlighted on the tent. Then he pressed ENTER.

"Yowlllll! Yowllll!" The recording screamed again and again.

A siren joined the noise. Red lights whirled outside as the security men issued their challenge against the unknown.

Thomas removed his fingers from the keyboard.

"Yowllll!" The hostile cry retreated. A distance growl sounded near the barn. It moved back toward the woods, and faded into the distance.

A pounding at the door of the camper caused everyone to jump.

GFF growled.

Thomas moved to the door but Martin eased him aside and opened it with caution.

"What was that?" The two security men asked as they pushed inside the crowded camper.

"Your lab called it a huge dog," Thomas answered.

"What about the blurry shadow of the boy?" The security men asked.

"My brother has yet to make an appearance." Pappy sighed.

"You mean this—thing—has something to do with the story you told? I thought you said your brother was dead."

Pappy nodded. "As dead as that Booger dog."

Somewhere in the distance a brilliant burst of fireworks color upstaged the electrical storm. Together they claimed the sky ritualizing freedom so dearly won by a hero named Pappy.

The security men were on duty outside. Everyone else was spending the night at Grandpa's cabin. The camper was finally quiet except for Grandpa's and GFF's snores and the excited whispers of David, who was finally getting to reveal the secret he'd kept for a lifetime.

"Being the grandson of a legend like Pappy DeMouse makes Super Heroes seem lame,"

David confided to Thomas. "Pappy's war stories were exciting. When I was older he told me about him, Dave, and Booger. It seemed unreal, like a fable."

"Did he really promise your mom he'd make everything right?" Thomas wondered.

"Yes, I don't know if he'd have come back except for that promise. He said being Pappy DeMouse was like play acting. This is real life and it's a lot harder."

Thomas hesitated. "Does he know what happened to Dave and Booger? He said they were dead!"

"I promised to never tell. But, you're going to hear it soon enough."

Thomas nodded, easing down on the bunk near David. He waited expectantly.

"Ringgg!"

Thomas grabbed for his cell phone before it woke Grandpa. He glanced at the caller ID and saw AHUNK, Sydney's ID.

"Hello Sydney! Did Kaylene . . ." Thomas began. He listened nodding his head, smiling, and looking at David with a I'll-tell-you-in-a-minute look.

"I'll fill in the rest when you and Kaylene bring Harley home in the morning," Thomas said. Once more he listened, nodding.

"Sure, he's right here with me." Thomas grinned at David. "You get some sleep, too. Tomorrow will be a big day. And the next day is the Fourth of July!"

"Harley, er, my great-grandpa is coming home tomorrow?" David asked excitedly.

"Yes! They checked him out. Sydney said to tell you the doctor confirmed Harley could run circles around a man half his age."

"Don't I know it? I played basketball against him, remember?

"Do you think it's too late to call Pappy? I bet he'll sleep a lot better knowing Harley's is fine and coming home tomorrow." He paused, "They didn't tell Harley about Pappy, did they?"

Thomas shook his head. "I'll call Martin's cell phone. He never goes to sleep until after the news." Thomas started to dial. "And, then, you're going to tell me the rest of the story, right?"

David nodded.

While David talked to Pappy, Thomas nudged GFF aside and looked out the camper window at the tent. The security car was parked near the entrance. All seemed quiet except for the fading drum roll of thunder. Ping! Ping! The music of rain on the metal roof of the camper orchestrated a symphony of promises for a bigger Fourth of July celebration.

"What's that noise, Thomas?" Grandpa growled.

"Rain! It's raining, Grandpa!" Thomas said.

Grandpa rolled over and sat up, rubbing his eyes. "Rain!" He glanced at the clock. "What time is it? And, what's David doing on the phone?"

"Sydney called. Harley's coming home tomorrow. We called to tell Pappy." A wide grin covered his face, "It's raining! And, David is going to tell me what happened to Dave and

Booger."

"I've got to hear this!" Grandpa said, just as David hung up.

David told the beginning of the story much as Harley and Grandpa told it. Now, he continued, ". . . Pappy, er Mick, said Booger turned on him! He said if his dad hadn't taken a stick to the dog the animal would have ripped his throat open." David stopped and swallowed hard.

"Mick said he heard someone holler, 'Fetch!' He thought it was Dave but it couldn't be because he'd fallen in the well. Booger heard it too, and let go. Mick said he knew if he didn't get up and run he'd never get away. He ran into the woods with Booger on his heels."

"Along the way, Mick picked up sticks. He threw them, hollering, 'Fetch!' The dog always went after the sticks but he always came back yelping and snarling."

"How did he finally get rid of Booger?" Thomas asked.

"He didn't. His friends, er, the gangsters he'd promised to run away, with killed Booger." David's eyes were wide. He said in an apologetic tone, "If they hadn't stopped the dog he would have killed Mick."

"Where were the gangsters?" Grandpa asked.

"Mick planned to meet them at the river. They were going by boat downstream where a car was waiting. They promised Mick big money to mechanic for them. He didn't know he would be fixing stolen cars until it was too late.

"Mick made it through the woods and the cemetery with Booger after him. He said he stumbled, rolled, and slid down the cliff path almost into the water. That's where the men were waiting. They stopped his fall."

David drew a deep breath. "Booger plunged after him. Mick said he was in pretty bad shape after Booger mauled him. The chase and the fall down the cliff path caused him to lose consciousness. When he opened his eyes he found himself lying on the ground near his brother, Dave.

"The men were working over his brother. Mick tried to get up and go to him but he was too weak. He heard one of the men ask how the boy got in the river.

"Mick told the men Dave fell in the well. One of them said the well must be fed by a spring that washed him into the river. That's when Mick saw Booger stretched out beside him. He knew the dog was dead. Mick passed out, again.

"When he woke up he was in the back seat of a car headed to Oklahoma. He asked what happened to his brother and Booger. One of the men told him the cemetery came in real handy. So, he always figured they buried them."

"Why didn't Mick try to get away and go back home?" Thomas asked.

"Mick was not much older than us. He'd been promised big money and was planning to run away anyway. He felt responsible for what happened to his brother and the dog. And, he thought his folks might blame him.

"The men blackmailed him into staying with them. They told him he could do jail time for what he did to his brother. They threatened to say Dave was still alive when they found him and Mick . . ."

"What a waste of a young life. Actually two young lives," Grandpa said.

"And, the dog. And Harley, and . . ." Thomas continued.

"Pappy said life is like a chain. It links everyone together. When one link is weak or gets broken, it ruins the whole chain."

"I think when Pappy became strong enough to break away from the bad guys and join the Air Force, he was on his way to helping forge a new link in that old chain," Grandpa said.

"Do you think when Pappy walked to the cemetery the other day he found where his brother and Booger were buried?" Thomas asked.

"I don't think so. He said the cemetery was overgrown with dry grass. He could hardly see the tombstones."

"That's the least of his worries now. Tomorrow, Harley's coming home. I hope Pappy finds the right way to tell his dad the story you just told us, David," Grandpa said.

"Maybe when all of this is over, we can clean up the cemetery and help find Dave's and Booger's grave."

An errie howl sounded from the back of Harley's property as if echoing Thomas's promise.

Chapter 16
July the Third

"Honk! Honk!" The sound of a horn woke Thomas. He glanced at the clock. 7:30 a.m. Were Sydney and Kaylene here with Harley already?

"Thomas, you and David, hurry out here and help us unload this truck." Grandpa pounded on the door of the camper.

The morning was crisp with the aftermath of rain. Vapor rose from the parched earth. The sun blistered its way into the new day promising the usual heat wave.

"It looks like we won't run out of fireworks," David said, stacking cases in the storage van.

"TNT makes sure of that," Thomas said.

Before they got the side curtains rolled up, cars were beginning to arrive.

"You guys hungry?" Wendy pushed through the crowd with sacks of food. As the day wore on, David and Thomas made their way to the storage trailer restocking shelves as customers continued to come.

Around noon, Sydney and Kaylene drove through heading toward Harley's house. The old man waved as they passed.

"Looks like Harley's okay," Thomas said, watching Pappy stare after the car.

Sydney worked his way through the crowd and came through into the tent. He went to

Pappy. "I want to assure you Harley is all right. In fact, he's in an argument with Kaylene about walking down here to check out the customers."

A grin started at the corner of Pappy's mouth. "That's the man I remember, hard headed as a mule."

Thomas whispered to David, "Don't worry, he'll find the right time to tell Harley."

"I know. He told me he's going to tell him tonight. I mentioned telling you and Grandpa about Dave and Booger last night. He said it would save him telling it."

"Martin, I met those security men as I turned off the highway," Sydney said. "They said they were going to drive to the road where you and Thomas were yesterday. They're going to find the maintenance road and cut through the back of Harley's farm to check out the shed near the cemetery."

Pappy exploded. "I wanted to go with them. If this crowd lets up I might walk back. It'll take them awhile to drive around there."

"It's a good thing TNT sent supplies. We're already running low. We may have to call for another truck tonight," Thomas said as he and David stopped to pat GFF on their way to the trailer for more stock. "You hot, boy?"

GFF looked wilted even in the shade but he favored them with an excited bark.

When they returned to the tent, Pappy was gone. They looked toward the woods and saw his red shirt just before he disappeared.

"Do you think he'll go to the house?"

Thomas asked.

"I don't think so. He said he wanted me and Lester with him when he told Harley," David said, stacking bottle rockets.

Cars covered the front parking lot. They began to fill the area behind the tent. People were prowling everywhere. They bought fireworks faster than the boys could keep the shelves stocked. They seemed confident the little bit of rain last night would make the chance of fire less.

Kaylene drove to the tent with Harley in the car to bring sandwiches. They had compromised. He could come if he promised to stay in the car. She hadn't counted on customers converging on the car to visit with him. She switched on the air. He talked for awhile before they drove back to his house taking GFF with them.

"Pow! Pow!"

"Was that fireworks or gunfire?" Thomas asked, looking toward the woods. Above the noise of the crowd, Thomas heard the sound of car motors racing somewhere at the back of the property. The racket continued toward the distant road where he and Martin had been yesterday.

Lester conferred with Martin. "I'd go check on Dad but I can hear him say, 'I can take care of myself. Take care of your job!'"

"He didn't have a gun, did he?" Martin asked.

Lester shook his head but without much conviction while customers kept them busy paying for products.

Late afternoon, one security man returned to the tent with Pappy. They explained how they'd discovered Jervis was holed up in the shed. They'd heard him and his wife arguing. His son wanted to shoot WONDERMAN.

Pappy looked at Thomas. "I guess that's the shell named after you, right?"

Thomas nodded. "That means they still have at least one load. I wonder if they have any of the ZEUS firecrackers?"

Pappy nodded. He explained how the wife accused Jervis of not keeping his promise about taking all the dogs back to the shelter. She heard a dog howling all night. He figured it was about the time Booger went back to the cemetery last night. His wife warned him if he didn't keep his word she'd leave him, again.

Pappy glanced at David and Thomas. "Jervis said he needed his medicine. He had a headache. If they didn't shut up they would be deader than the boy and dog the kid was telling about last night. And, he'd make sure that boy, Thomas, and his terrier mutt joined them."

"How did he know, David . . .?" Thomas began. He broke off looking at Grandpa and David. He knew by the looks on their faces they were thinking the same thing as him—Jervis and his family had been outside the camper last night listening when David told Pappy's story.

"He was listening, wasn't he?" Grandpa said, "And, he mentioned Thomas and GFF?"

Pappy nodded. "Where is the terrier?"

Wendy had been listening without an word. Now, she gasped, "Kaylene took GFF with her and Harley!"

"I better go check on them." Sydney took off in a run toward the house.

"When I heard him mention Thomas and the dog, I started to go in but Jervis heard the security men's car," Pappy said. "He and his family must have dashed out the door by the pickup. I heard him yell, 'get down!'"

"That's why we only saw him when the pick-up tore out from behind the shed heading right at us. We swerved into a ditch trying to avoid him. Then we shot into the air hoping to slow him down. That's where Pappy found us."

Pappy nodded. "We checked the area with no luck. We thought we better let you know what was happening."

The fireworks crew heard the story as they continued to help customers.

Martin leaned closer and asked the security man, "Where is your partner?"

Pappy grinned. "We left him to guard the shed. Jervis will be back because the fireworks shell, the firecrackers, and his medicine are still there. That's our bait. He sounded like he needed the medicine real bad. And, if that boy wants to shoot WONDERMAN, Jervis will have to come back and get the shell and load. The mother will make sure of that."

"So, if Sydney watches Kaylene, Harley and GFF, you watch me, and the security man watches the shed, we can take care of this tent and sell fireworks to celebrate the big holiday tomorrow," Thomas summed it up wiping sweat from his face.

"I'll help watch you, Thomas, cause I'm your assistant manager, remember?" Wendy promised.

Thomas gave her a quick hug and hurried to restock the smoke bombs.

Dusk settled over the Jones farm necessitating lights that illuminated the tent. Early celebrations were beginning in the distance as fireworks lit up the skies over Branson.

Sydney drove Kaylene, Harley, and GFF to town and picked up pizza to feed the crew. When they returned, Sydney honked and motioned for Thomas to bring someone and get the food.

"Come with me, Pappy. You, Lester, David, and I, should be able to take care of this, right?" Thomas smiled.

They looked at Pappy. He nodded and moved toward the parked car. GFF yipped when he saw Thomas and David. He jumped from the back seat to the front until Kaylene handed him outside to Thomas. He was instantly quiet in Thomas's arms.

"Harley, you remember David?" Thomas motioned toward his friend.

Harley nodded, looking beyond the red-haired boy to the men accompanying him. "And, who are these gentlemen?"

"This is the famous World War Two ace, Pappy, 'Mick' DeMouse, David's grandpa." Thomas's eyes widened as he realized he'd used Pappy's given name. He hurried on, "And, this is Lester, who is retired from the Marines, David's father."

Harley studied the two men and settled on Pappy. "Your eyes look familiar, sir. Have we met before?"

"It's been a long time. I've got a story . . ." Pappy began.

"Fire! Fire!" Shouts came from the side of the tent nearest the maintenance road.

Clutching GFF, Thomas ran to the back of the tent. He cried out, "Fire, it's headed this way."

GFF yipped.

Pappy ran to look and hurried back to the car. "Watch after Harley and Kaylene, Sydney. The house is probably the safest place. The fire will have to get past here to get to it. We'll have it stopped before then."

Harley put a hand out the window pointing to the barn. "Take care of the barn!"

Pappy nodded. He watched the car pull through the departing crowd. Customers were fleeing like rats deserting a sinking ship as the fire moved in a steady line across the dry grass field toward the fireworks tent.

Martin, David, and Thomas ran from the tent. Their arms were loaded with cases of fireworks. They headed toward the storage trailer.

GFF yipped excitedly. He raced around and around the pole where his lease rope was attached.

Lester hollered, "Come on, Dad. Let's help get the fireworks out of the tent. They've called the fire department. If all else fails we can hook the trailer behind the Land Rover and move the explosives.

Grandpa cleared counters into boxes and directed his crews as they removed products from the tent. Many of the male customers returned to help after they'd moved their vehicles and families to safety.

"Look at that fire move! Who'd have thought sparks from fireworks could start something like this inferno," Lester shouted.

"I doubt it was started by sparks," Martin said. "It extends from one end of the field to the other like it was set."

Sirens moved closer. Fire trucks rumbled onto the Jones farm and moved toward their enemy as it moved closer and closer to the fireworks tent and the barn.

"That's the last of the fireworks. Do you think we should drop the tent? Or move the tables?" Thomas asked, moping sweat.

Grandpa was soaked with fatigue. He wiped his eyes and turned his gaze toward the fire. "Hook the camper onto my pickup. The storage trailer cab can pull itself, if needed."

"I've got all the baskets moved." Wendy puffed.

The fire department torched the grass in front of a trench they plowed across the field. The trench separated the rest of Harley's field from the rampaging fire on the move.

A cheer went up from the crowd parked along the road.

"They're using a back-fire!" Thomas shouted, "It'll cause the main fire to burn itself out when they reach each other."

"They're getting it under control. Let's leave the tent and tables," Grandpa said.

Pappy sighed, "That means the barn is safe, not to mention the house, and the people inside."

"It had to be Jervis and his family who set the fire. It probably wasn't fireworks. Their fireworks are in the shed . . ." Martin began.

"The shed!" Thomas shouted. "Jervis must have set the fire as a diversion to get to the shed. Martin, we've got to get back there. Could we cut across by the barn and hit the maintenance road? It would take us to the shed."

Martin nodded. He motioned to the security man. "I bet your partner can use some help." Martin jumped into the cab of the pickup he'd borrowed for the season. "Thomas, grab GFF. You, David, and Wendy get up front with me. Anyone else who's going, get in the back. Hold on! It'll be a rough ride."

Chapter 17
Fetch!

Lester and Pappy crawled in the Land Rover. "Ride with us, Tom."

"I've got to stay here and watch the merchandise," Grandpa said.

"Go on, man. We'll watch it for you." Grandpa looked up to see a group of men he'd known as boys in Branson. They'd renewed friendship during the fireworks season and returned to help with the fire.

"Leave us the keys, Tom. If the fire gets too close we'll move the camper and the storage trailer."

Grandpa tossed his friend the keys. "Take care of everything. TNT will have my hide if you don't."

The vehicles moved across the pasture to the barn and headed for the woods beyond. The fire gave false light which was dimmed as they moved onto the path leading between the trees.

"I'm going to call Sydney and tell him what's going on," Thomas said.

Martin nodded, switching on his headlights.

Thomas's cell rang as soon as he hung up. He checked the ID. "Mom? Are you okay?" Thomas asked.

Martin and Wendy looked anxiously at Thomas.

"You're fine." He nodded his assurance. "A message? Well, Martin's . . ." He stopped abruptly as Martin gave him a warning look. He knew it meant to not upset his mom.

"Sure, Mom. I'll tell him." Thomas listened intently, nodding, frowning, his eyes darting from one face to another as he concentrated on what his mom said. "He's got to have the medicine to keep from going off the deep end?"

Martin switched off his lights and moved slowly along the rough road leading toward the shed. The security man, who had been standing in the back of the pickup tapped on the back cab window and pointed to the shed.

"There it is. The green pickup!" Wendy nudged David, who nodded.

Thomas continued his conversation, "All of them? His son, Roy and his wife, Molly? How can that be? People heard them. He—what? Wait a minute, Mom." Thomas put his hand over the cell. "Martin, you've got to listen."

Martin held up a detaining finger as he pulled onto the cemetery road. He parked the pickup in sight of the cliff road and the river. "Stay here!" he commanded. Jumping out, he and the security man zigzagged between tombstones as they raced through the tall grass. They climbed into the Land Rover which took off in the direction of the shed. Their tail lights blinked in the twilight.

"What is it, Thomas?" Wendy said, holding GFF closer.

Thomas shook his head. He was trying to understand the doctor's report his mom was reading him. "The doctor believes Jervis hates me and GFF because he confused us with Roy and his little dog that jumped on him when he lost control of his car and pulled in front of the semi?"

"Yowlll!" The sound came from the woods moving toward the cemetery.

"It's Booger!" David said, "Pappy knew he'd return."

"Yip! Yip Yip!" GFF struggled from Wendy's grasp and moved onto David's lap near the passenger window. He jumped up and put his paws on the window and begin to growl.

"What is it, GFF?" Wendy begged.

Thomas edged behind the steering wheel gaining assurance from the warmth of Martin that still remained. "Mom, I think I got it all. I'll tell Martin. Yes, I'll be careful. I love you, too." He hung up.

"Thomas!" David jerked Wendy closer to him as he stared at the window behind Thomas. "He's out there!"

Before Thomas could turn, someone began pounding on the window with a force that rocked the pickup.

"Yowlll!" The cry was closer.

Wendy whimpered.

GFF jumped from David's lap, crossed Wendy's jean-clad legs, and onto Thomas's thighs. Putting his nose to the window glass, he growled.

Slowly, Thomas turned.

Jervis stood beside the pickup holding the WONDERMAN tube and a fireworks load in one hand. In the other hand he held a butane torch. "Get out, Roy. Bring the dog with you!"

"Mister, you're sick. Your wife and son are dead. I'm not—" Thomas began.

Instantly, Jervis's face contorted. Thomas peered into the near darkness thinking he saw a woman. He heard her voice, "Jervis, I warned you about hurting our son."

Jervis seemed to shrivel becoming smaller. His face appeared as a boy. A voice whined, "You promised! You've got the fireworks. Let me shoot them."

"What's happening?" David whispered.

"He's crazy enough to kill. Humor him, stay inside, lock the . . ." Thomas warned as though reciting from the doctor's report.

"Thomas, lock your—" Wendy said, just as the door was jerked open.

Jervis grabbed Thomas by the arm and jerked him outside, slamming the door, but not before GFF jumped out, too.

GFF attached himself to Jervis's trouser leg, yanking and growling.

Jervis yelled, kicking out trying to free himself of the dog. GFF landed in a heap near a gravestone.

Thomas was facing Jervis. He could see the outline of the Land Rover moving slowly forward on the path behind the man. Behind the Land Rover loomed a dark image moving in cadence.

"Here, take the fireworks. Shoot them! Before your mother goes away, again." Jervis pushed the tube and load into Thomas's hands. "Do it, now!" He handed Thomas the butane lighter.

Thomas stared at the man who had lost his wife and son in an automobile accident. What was it his mom said? "Their voices are inside him. He believes they are alive because they talk through him. Thomas, he is three people. Be careful."

"I can't see. It's too dark. I need light." Thomas made his voice whine like the voice he'd heard when the boy named Roy spoke.

"Whiner! Light the torch. Shoot the fireworks before your mother leaves," Jervis commanded, arm upraised to strike.

Thomas flicked the torch and held it toward the man who would strike him.

Jervis moved back assuming the woman's pose. "Roy, be careful. You'll get burned." Posturing, with his head tilted backward, he assaulted the silence of the cemetery with his crazed laughter.

The fireworks fuse dangled loosely from Thomas's arm. He set the tube down and anchored it against a gravestone near GFF. Moving swiftly, he torched the long fuse. It ignited, beginning to burn toward the point of impact. "Lights! Noise!" Thomas yelled as he reached to pick up GFF.

The cemetery was flooded with light as the Land Rover's headlights caught Jervis, Thomas, and GFF like startled deer in their glare. David turned on the pickup lights which paved a luminous path toward the cliff edge. He began to sound the pickup horn. Behind them, the Land Rover's horn blared. Beside the Land Rover another set of headlights flashed and a horn blasted.

Jervis grabbed his head as voices screamed from his lips changing from mother to son and back again.

"Yowlll!" Rising from behind the Land Rover a humongous shadow leaped forward and hovered over the crazed Jervis.

The voice of Roy screamed. Jervis's body, hosting three people, began to run down the lighted path made from the pickup lights.

Thomas stared in horror as he backed toward the pickup. He didn't realize the fireworks tube had attached itself to his jeans.

"Thomas, your leg!" A chorus of male voices yelled from beyond the light.

"Yowlll!" The shadow moved toward Thomas.

Reaching down, Thomas grabbed the fuse between the lit end and the load and flung it toward the cliff yelling, "Fetch, Booger!"

The WONDERMAN load ignited as it went over the cliff. The humongous shadow followed it. A flash of color lit up the sky just beyond the space where Jervis stood. Fireballs soared into the heavens. Millions of lights swirled, forming the giant outline of a super hero.

Thomas sucked in his breath as he watched Jervis, like a puppet on a string, dance a duel of destruction as he faced WONDERMAN, the mighty warrior.

Thomas felt pressure on all sides of him and realized Martin, Lester, Pappy, David, and Wendy, and the two security men, flanked him like sentinels. They were joined by Sydney,

Kaylene, and Harley.

Presto! Another fireball exploded in front of WONDERMAN and became an opponent with weapon raised. Jervis stepped toward the edge of the cliff.

"Jervis! Come back!" Thomas yelled.

GFF echoed the warning with a yelp.

Bolts of fire erupted from WONDERMAN's extended arm flashing across space to eliminate the enemy.

A smile of delight spread across Jervis's face as Roy yelled, "Thanks Dad! I love you."

A woman's serene voice echoed over the cemetery, "Come, Jervis, let's take Roy home."

"Wait!" The fireworks crew yelled.

As WONDERMAN's opponent cascaded downward in bursts of color, Jervis stepped forward over the cliff.

Silence descended over the cemetery.

Sydney put a protective arm across Thomas's shoulder. "There was nothing anyone could do. Jervis was a walking time bomb."

Recognizing his friend's voice, Thomas exclaimed, "Sydney, Kaylene, how did you get here! Where's Harley?"

"We talked to Martin on his cell. When we found out Jervis was here, we came."

"I'd been trying to tell them I needed to check out that shed," Harley grouched.

Pappy moved toward Harley bringing with him Lester and David. "Remember, I promised you a story, old man?"

Harley stared at the two men and boy outlined by headlights. He squinted, his eyes widened, and a question formed in the distance between them. "I can't believe . . . " His voice broke. "Your eyes, so much like your ma's . . . " In a choked voice, he chanted,

"It's been lonely here in Branson, Missouri,
On this hilly, curvy road.
With just a donkey, a pig,
And an old horny toad.
It's beautiful country
But no one, much, around.
So, we raised our voices
In a joyful sound . . ."

Pappy closed the distance between him and his father reciting the rest of the long ago, remembered poem, "Oink, oink, croak, hee haw." He gathered the old man close against him crooning, "Dad, Dad."

Harley murmured, "Mick, it's my boy, Mick."

Lester and David joined the family hug.

Thomas brushed his eyes with his hand as he heard Wendy whisper, "Are you crying, Thomas? I am."

"Yowlll!" The cry rose from the depths of the cliff. The shadow leapt up and over the edge, coming directly toward them. In the midst of it was a flare of fire like a burning stick. It moved toward them returning the fetched prize.

Thomas remembered the words, "Booger always came back with the stick." He reached down and picked up the butane torch. He pitched it to David. "I don't think Booger will be satisfied until he fetches for a Jones."

While the crew ran for their vehicles, David flicked the butane light. It flared. He threw it with all his might toward the other end of the cemetery. He yelled, "Fetch! Booger! Fetch!"

The shadow moved after the arch of fire as the vehicles roared toward the maintenance road. Near the woods, they stopped, staring in disbelief as the tall grass caught fire and burned toward them.

"Look Martin! There's a ditch running along the road on the cemetery side. Can we make our own back fire?" Thomas shouted.

"Lester, drive to the end of the road by the shed. Light the grass on the other side of the ditch there. We'll do the same along here." Martin gestured to Thomas and they ran to light the grass at their end. It flamed and moved toward its twin, swallowed it, and roared toward the edge of the cliff.

"Good thinking, boy! The fire will burn itself out and over the edge," Harley said.

"Look!" Thomas pointed toward the far edge of the cemetery near the cliff.

A black cloud of smoke billowed upward from the flames. Rising from its midst, a dark shadow took on the image of a phantom dog. It blazed across the star-studded sky in pursuit of a slight blurry image. Colliding, the two merged in pyrotechnic splendor. Then, the apparition burst into molecules of brilliance, spiraling higher and higher until it disappeared into the heavens.

"Rest In Peace, Dave and Booger. It's your

turn to fly the skies. I'm finally home to take care of Pa." Pappy sighed, clasping his father's arm and turning him toward the Land Rover. "Come ride with me, Dad. I've got a story you've been waiting to hear for a long time."

Chapter 18
Fourth of July

"Wake up, GFF! It's the Fourth of July!" Thomas jumped out of bed. "Come on David, The truck will be here soon. We need to help Grandpa unload."

GFF bounded out of bed yipping.

"Is it morning all ready?" David rubbed his eyes. "Man, we just got to bed."

"I know! If you, your dad, Sydney, and all of Grandpa's friends, hadn't stayed to help us put the fireworks back in the tent we'd still be working." Thomas grabbed a cereal box and milk preparing for breakfast on the run.

"Last night seems like a dream," David said, "Pappy telling Harley everything and then staying with him last night. Just think it had been over sixty years since Pappy slept in his own room."

"Some parts were like a dream, others were more like a nightmare." Thomas scooped another bite.

"It was unreal. Tell me one more time about Jervis, Roy, and Molly. It's hard to believe he's dead."

"Jervis was one sick dude." Thomas poured GFF some milk in a bowl. "When he wrecked his car and his wife and son died, he refused to believe they were dead." Thomas offered David the cereal box. "Jervis recreated his lost family inside his mind where they could live through him. But, when he took his medicine they would leave. Then, he'd remember the accident and blame Roy and the dog. He thought they were the cause of Molly leaving him."

"When Dad and I came to the shelter, I never understood why he was so mean to the dogs," David said, "Now, I understand. He was blaming them for the accident, too."

"Poor GFF." Thomas reached to stroke the terrier's ear. "Jervis really had it in for him. I'm glad we adopted him when we did."

"That may be why Jervis came after you," David said.

"That, and the idea that we caused him to lose his job." Thomas carried his empty bowl to the sink. "I think that was about the time he started believing I was Roy and GFF was Roy's dog."

"It's weird how everyone thought his wife and son were still with him," David said.

"In a way they were—right up to the very end," Thomas said.

Honk! Honk!

"Let get going. There's the truck." Thomas grabbed GFF and made for the door.

"Look at Harley's farm. It looks like a charcoal drawing," Thomas said, as he carried the last case of fireworks into the tent.

Grandpa said, "The grass will grow back. And, the cemetery should have been burned off a long time ago. It'll make it easier to find Dave and Booger's grave."

"Can we really come down when I get back from the AAU tournament and help them search for Dave and Booger's grave?"

"They invited us, didn't they?" Grandpa continued rolling up side curtains. "Of course, they may have already found them by then, but we'll certainly come down for the ceremony when they bury them properly."

"Meanwhile, let's get this place opened. Customers will be here before . . . " He chuckled. "Can you believe this is the last morning I'll have to say that?"

"At least until next year." Thomas grinned.

Grandpa groaned. "Give an old man a vacation, will you? Let's don't even think about next year for at least a month or two. These old bones need some reast."

"Rest doesn't have an 'a' in it, Grandpa," Thomas admonished.

"I know. But, it makes it sound longer." Grandpa chuckled.

Sydney and Kaylene drove up, followed by a line of cars.

"Here they come, Grandpa. We better get ready!" Thomas ran to secure GFF to his tether pole while David carried another case to the storage trailer.

Sydney jumped out waving a newspaper. "You made the news again, Wonderman."

"I think I've been here before." Grandpa grumbled, "My grandson's head is going to be so big it won't fit in his Black Cat T-shirt."

"What . . . ?" Thomas said, just as Martin pulled the pickup to a stop near the camper. Lester and Wendy went into the camper carrying baskets and boxes.

"Don't look now, Thomas, but I think

we've got a special visitor!" Grandpa said.

Thomas looked toward the trailer, "Mom! I didn't know you were coming!" He bounded across the space and caught his mom in a big hug.

"I just couldn't stay away. I was so afraid for you. But I had to tell you about Jervis and his problems. When I hung up, I was so nervous I had to do something. So, I started cooking." She hugged him tighter. "I made all your favorites. When Martin called to say you were okay. I told him I was coming down and bringing food for a Fourth of July picnic."

"Mom, are you sure you and the baby are okay?" Thomas asked.

"I'm not sick. I'm just expecting. If it gets too hot I'll go in the camper and cool off. Meanwhile, we're going to have a bang-up picnic for Independence Day."

"Thomas, when you get through hugging your mom, I need some help," Grandpa hollered.

As the sun beat down on the fireworks tent, the Fourth of July crowd arrived. They continued to come throughout the morning. Soon the whole fireworks crew were at their stations restocking, handing out baskets, and making changes for customers.

Harley joined Carol and Kaylene as they busied themselves getting the Fourth of July picnic ready.

"Ringgg!" Thomas picked up his cell phone. The caller ID showed TNT.

"Hi, TNT." Thomas smiled. "Yes, the truck

got here."

Grandpa motioned he wanted to talk.

Thomas waved him off with a grin. "T-shirts?"

Grandpa slapped an open palm against his forehead and reached beneath the counter pulling out a box. He held up a red T-shirt with a Black Cat logo on the front. Arched around the Black Cat's head in script was Rainbow Fireworks."

Thomas gave Grandpa a thumbs-up signal. "Wow! The T-shirts are cool!"

"Wonderman, I figured if you're going to continue to make headlines you might as well be a billboard and advertise." She paused, "When are you leaving for Florida?"

"Day after tomorrow."

"You've done a fine job as manager, Thomas. We'll settle up when you get back, okay?"

"Sure, I've already decided to put my pay in my college fund. Thanks, TNT."

"Don't mention it. Let me talk to your grandpa."

"Okay, say hello to Lefty. I can't wait for him to see my dog, General Freddie Freedom."

"Mighty impressive name. Must be an impressive dog."

"Just wait until you see him!" Thomas bragged.

Grandpa handed Thomas a T-shirt. "Better put this on. It looks like the television crew is back to interview the boy-hero!"

"Grandpa!" Thomas admonished, but he quickly skinned out of his shirt and donned the

Black Cat T-shirt.

People gathered around as the television crew prepared for an interview. Martin, Lester, Sydney, and David, insisted on staying in the tent to help customers.

Grandpa, Wendy, and Thomas stood waiting for the interview in their new fireworks T-shirts.

Thomas whispered to Grandpa, "TNT was right. We will be advertising for her."

Grandpa nodded, embarrassed at so much attention.

Wendy waved at Carol, Kaylene, and Harley, who were enjoying the show. Then she hollered, "Wait!" She ran to untie GFF and returned with him in her arms. "Here, Thomas, you hold General Freddie Freedom."

"Yip, yip-yip!" GFF announced.

The television reporter smiled. "You're right, General, we need to get this show on the road." And she began, "This is Stella Stiles reporting from Branson, Missouri. We're at the fireworks tent on the Harley Jones farm where Thomas Scott and his crew have once more been the center of excitement . . ."

Grandpa nudged Thomas, who suppressed a grin.

" . . . Neither fire, stalkers, or the resolution of a sixty year-old mystery can stay these fireworks contractors from providing the means for people to celebrate this special day."

The camera man had just spotted something on the back of Thomas's T-shirt, he panned in on it.

Stella glanced quickly at the logo. Her eyes brightened and she said, "Thomas, these are unique T-shirts. If your grandpa will turn around I'd like for you to read the quote on the back of his shirt."

Thomas studied the back of Grandpa's shirt, then he began to read, "I am apt to believe that it will be celebrated by succeeding generations with illuminations (Fireworks), from one end of this continent to the other. . . forevermore! John Adams, July 4, 1776."

GFF yipped! Then reached up to lick Thomas's face. The flag on his collar caught the light.

"Thomas, your dog is excited about the Fourth of July, too, isn't he?" Stella smiled reaching to pat GFF.

Thomas grinned as GFF gave Stella a big lick on the face. "I think General Freddie Freedom is agreeing with Mister Adams. We're still celebrating our freedom on Independence Day with fireworks. Now, I think it's time to get back and wait on our customers, don't you, Grandpa and Wendy?"

They both nodded. Wendy smiled into the camera and waved as Stella Stiles wrapped up her story to the tune of the national anthem.

"This is Stella Stiles, with our guest, Thomas Scott, and his family and friends, who join me in wishing you and yours a happy Fourth of July from Boomland, Branson, Missouri, USA.

The End

How to Order
The Land Series of Books
With Mollycoddles® Toys

• The Land Series of Books and the Mollycoddles® line of Companion Toys are available through many bookstores, but are also available directly from the publisher:

Jane Hale
Rainbow Publications
45 Rocket Road
Buffalo, Missouri 65622
(417) 345-7759 / phone & fax
email: jshale@ripinternet.com

• You may call or email your order using a credit card or you may photocopy one of the order forms on the next few pages and mail in your order with a check or credit card information.

• Telephone, fax and email orders okay with complete credit card information, including number, exp. date, address and telephone number.

• Missouri residents please add 7% sales tax.

• Items marked "NYA" are "Not Yet Available" as of the first printing of this book. However, all of them are expected to be available by the year 2005, if not well before.

ORDER FORM

		Qty	Total
Wonderland - A Christmas Mystery	$9.95	____	_____
ISBN 0-934426-79-1			
Ringo Reindeer	8.95	____	_____
Heartland - A Valentine Mystery	12.95	____	_____
ISBN 0-934426-91-0			
Rascal the Cyber-Rat	7.95	____	_____
Foreverland - An Easter Mystery	12.95	____	_____
ISBN 0-934426-95-3			
Cackleberry Chick (before the egg)	8.95	____	_____
Boomland - A 4th-of-July Mystery	12.95	____	_____
ISBN 0-934426-20-1			
Freddie Freedom	9.98	____	_____
Spookyland - A Halloween Mystery	NYA	____	_____
ISBN			
Mollycoddles® Companion Toy	NYA	____	_____
Homeland - A Thanksgiving Mystery	NYA	____	_____
ISBN			
Mollycoddles® Companion Toy	NYA	____	_____

Tax (Mo residents please add 7%)   _____

Shipping: $3 for 1st item, $1 per additional item.   _____

T O T A L   _____

❑ Check Enclosed.   ❑ Please charge to my Credit Card.

❑ Visa   ❑ MasterCard   ❑ Discover   ❑ American Express

Card No._____exp_____

Name_____

Address_____

_____

Phone_____